Plucked

Book two of Feathered Dreams

By: Brittany Putzer

Plucked

Editor: Kat Pagan
Cover by Rae Lumpkins
ISBN: 978-0-578-83916-5

Published in the United States.

Dedication

To God, who gave me this wonderful imagination and stubborn strong will to conjure this book series. Also, to my lovely family and friends. Your love has helped me soar to unimaginable heights. I will be forever grateful for your love and support.

#PutzerReadingTribe

Contents

The Mess Within

I squint into the empty, black pipe and groan loudly. "Okay, try it again, Dan!"

I hear muffled, heavy footsteps, as the contractor goes to the water faucet. All of a sudden, my face is assaulted with brown sludge and gritty debris. I sputter and spit loudly while rubbing my cheek. Then clear running water starts flowing freely. The husky laughter behind me is audible as the construction workers watch me struggle. I stand and shake it off. "Well, boys. It is working now."

Dan walks over, his green eyes sparkling. "Sorry, Ann. The water pipe must have been clogged."

"Well, that is just one problem fixed on our list, Dan." I continue to wipe my face and look around the newly built chicken pen and yard. The smell of fresh cut wood gets caught in the cool afternoon breeze. I close my eyes and take a deep breath in.

Only a month has passed since King Mark suddenly died in his sleep. It feels like a lifetime ago. A lot has happened since then. The funeral was a significant public ordeal. The royal family required everyone's assistance getting it together, especially that of King Mark's mourning wife, Elizabeth.

Elizabeth had found her husband dead in his bed early that morning. Since she never knew of her husband's evil intentions, the loss was a great one to her. I stood by her, like the daughter she always wanted. I made sure she was taken care of and that everything ran smoothly.

The young Princes, Ryan and Christian, had the Coronation to plan and execute. They both studied and prepared for the big event, which was the day after their father's funeral. Even though their father was not necessarily the nicest, I could tell they were hurt over his death. Especially when they saw how it affected their mother. Both of them were very patient with her. Their love for her had no bounds and that made my heart soar with pride.

The love triangle between the Princes and me is confusing to say the least. Most of the time, when we were together, Christian seemed withdrawn. While Ryan seemed carefree. But that was because of their father. He demanded Christian choose Mary and send me home. Which he did, but Ryan came with me and a relationship started to blossom. Then we returned to the Palace because Ryan needed emergency surgery. King Mark tried to send me home again by threatening me and my family. The night that I was sure he was going to kill me, he died in his sleep. Now I am trying to do whatever is needed of me, here at the Palace. While simultaneously trying to forget what I had with each of them and move on.

But that is easier said than done.

I shake the memories from my thoughts and stare out in front of me. The project I had started a few months ago (to help boost egg and meat production with the Palace's chickens) was now almost complete. I sigh and step back. I admire the hard work that was done to transform it from a caged barn to a free-range run and coop.

I hear soft footsteps behind me and turn to see Christian's assistant, Tim, walking over. His dark eyes are sparkling, as he assesses my watery situation.

"Lady Ann. King Christian requires your immediate attention."

I look down at my drenched pants and cock a brow at him. "He said immediately?"

He nods and smirks at me. I groan inwardly and grab his outstretched arm. I turn and smile at Dan and his crew.

"I hope you guys have a good night. You've earned it. I will see you all again tomorrow, *bright and early.*"

They all smile as they start cleaning up their tools and materials. I grin as I watch them, knowing their Christmas bonus will be greatly appreciated. I took my pay and split it amongst the crew for their hard work and dedication. I do not need it at the moment, and I know their families could use it for the holidays.

I sigh as we walk inside the Palace. My eyes twinkle, as I watch the maids hang Christmas decorations. There was tinsel, wreaths, and many twinkling, bright lights sprawled all over. It makes my eyes water as memories of my mom's favorite holiday pass through my mind. My heart feels heavy knowing this would be another holiday without her.

As we ascend the stairs to the third floor, I take a steadying breath. My encounters with Christian always take a toll on me. Even though we haven't been in a relationship for a few months, I still feel an electric current when he is near. Tim knocks on Christian's office door. We walk in, and Tim releases my arm and smirks towards Christian.

"Your highness. Lady Ann is here to see you."

Christian lifts his brilliant blue eyes off the papers he is scanning. He drops the pen he is holding as his gaze drifts across my body. "My goodness, Lady Ann, you must have had a busy day." He sets the papers down and leans back. He nods towards Tim. "Thank you, Tim. You're excused."

"Ann, dare I even ask, why are you all wet? What happened to you?"

I run my hand through my wet chestnut hair. "King Christian, it's the new fashion. What do you think?" I bat my lashes.

I see laughter sparkling behind his tired eyes. "Does this new fashion involve every man being able to see through your shirt? Plus, bonus, almost through your bra?" He quirks a brow.

I look down and examine myself more closely. Crap! My white shirt is now see-through, and the light grey bra is not helping the situation. I shrug as my face pinkens. "I was going to change but you said you wanted to see me *immediately*."

Christian rubs his face. "Yes, I did say that." He sighs. "Thank you for coming quickly, Ann. Would you please have a seat." He motions for the chair positioned in front of his desk.

I rub my hands on the back of my jeans, and dirt speckles the floor. "Never mind sitting, Ann. You can walk around the desk and get closer. That way I don't have to shout."

This shirt was a big mistake. His eyes start to glaze with a smoldering look. He clears his throat and redirects his attention to my face. "The autopsy came back for my father and unfortunately, he passed from a heart attack."

I watch him strain to read the words. I place a hand on his shoulder. Then I offer a tissue from his desk. He grabs my hand and holds it in his warm one. "The report goes on to say that they are waiting for blood and tissue sample results. They haven't been able to rule out poison."

My blood runs cold. Is that even feasible with all the guards and precautions the Palace takes? It would be difficult to track the murderer down now after all this time.

"I'm sorry, Christian. This must feel like salt in the wound. Have you told your mom or Ryan?"

He squeezes my fingers and then releases them, freeing himself to put the papers in the safe. "I told Ryan this morning, but not mom. Until I have hard evidence, I don't want to make the situation any tougher for her."

"Christian, why did you tell me? I mean, I'm grateful you have confided in me, but I'm not sure why."

He stands up and I hear his spine pop as he leans back. Then he turns to me and touches the jeweled band on my finger as his eyes glaze over. "You're still wearing the ring I gave you."

I look down at the beautiful diamond with a chicken in the middle of it. The ring was made for our engagement before the King demanded Christian marry Lady Mary. Christian gave it to me as a parting gift.

"Why wouldn't I wear it? Was it meant to be locked away?"

His eyes turn dark for a moment. "I'd understand if you never wore it because of all the awful memories it represents."

"Christian. Not all of those memories were awful." I run my hand over his forearm before turning to walk out. Christian gently grabs my arm and steps closer. I inhale sharply as he bends his face close to mine. Why did he have to smell amazing?

He rests his forehead on mine, then he whispers, "For goodness' sake, Ann. Please put a jacket on before leaving here."

I push him away. "I can't magically produce one, Christian."

He grabs his suit jacket off his coat rack and helps me in it, taking his time putting it on. "Ann, go straight to your room and change. Then come back to my office. I have another job for you." I feel him brush my wet hair aside and tingles run down my spine. His words sink in and my eyes go wide.

"Oh, no, you don't!" I turn on my heels. "Don't think you can butter me up."

He groans and sits back in his chair as I corner him, glaring. "Christian. You promised I could go home and see my dad."

"Well, you can't blame me for trying to keep you here longer. I need all the help I can get right now."

7

"Christian, you have *always* needed all kinds of help but I'm serious. It has been a while, and I miss him."

"Come on, Ann, give me a few more weeks."

"Weeks," I squeak out.

I kneel in front of him, making him look me in the eyes.

"I remember what I told you. But, Ann, please have mercy on me." He runs his hand down my face and cups my chin.

I shake him off and stand up.

"Christian, you have your fiancée to help you." Then I turn to leave, my face red.

"Don't make me beg, Ann."

His pleading voice pulls at my heart and I stop.

He continues to stroke my ego. "I can't confide in Mary like I can with you. I can pay you more and promise you extravagant gifts, but I know that you aren't materialistic. So, tell me, what do you want? At this time, I need to be surrounded by friends and family that I trust. It won't be forever. You have my word."

"First, I need you to stop pretending to be attracted to me because you are my friend and nothing else. Next, I want you to bring my dad here for a special vacation and treat him like the king that he is."

He hugs me tight. "Bringing your father to the Palace is a wonderful idea. It'll give me a chance to get to know him, and he can put you in your place like nobody else can." He pulls back and watches me. "Ann, the feelings I have for you are the same as they were. They're not easily turned off."

I stare into his eyes, waiting for the punchline. "Well, you need to get over that, it's in the past. All I want from you is friendship." I look away. "I'm curious as to what has changed? I mean, we haven't so much as touched the last few weeks and now all of a sudden—"

He pushes me towards the threshold. "How about you try to not flash me the next time you come in here." He opens the door. "I'll work on bringing your father here for a king's vacation. Thank you, Ann, I appreciate all that you are doing for us. Now change and come back, please."

Fall had always been my favorite time of year and dad made it unique. Especially after my mom died. He would volunteer to put up a Christmas tree, lights, and make my favorite meals. He made every effort to keep a smile on my face. Even if that meant freezing outside while we construct snow hens. It'll be nice having him close by, even if it is at the Palace and not our home. I make a mental note to call him later to check on the ladies and hear his voice.

When I close the door to my room, I see Karen putting away clothes, her maid uniform starched and not a hair out of place. Our relationship started off with her being my maid, and now she is my best friend.

Her eyes sweep over my unholy mess and she starts laughing.

"It's not funny, Karen. Everyone saw me like this," I groan. "I blame Dan."

"Dan's sweet and he would never do that to you on purpose."

"Whose side are you on? What happened to hoes over bros?"

A towel flies at my face. "As your fellow hoe, I need to tell you, you need to shower."

"I wish I had time to shower. Christian needs me back in his office. Just grab me a simple dress and flats, please."

"Christian is working you to the bone with all of his requests. Can't he ask Mary or his cute assistant for help?"

"Aren't you married to Vinny? Plus, Tim isn't into women."

She pokes her head out of my closet. "What? No way."

"Yes, Tim is perfectly happy with his boyfriend Jay."

She groans and starts tossing stuff on my bed for me. I dress then look in the mirror, and I'm met by a bright-eyed chicken queen with a nest on her head. Karen helps me finish taming my hair with a French braid, laying it across my shoulder. She affixes light feather earrings to my ears and a little heart necklace across my chest. She grabs the makeup out of my drawer, but I put up a hand.

"I would rather not."

She shrugs and sets the concealer down. "If you want to walk around with those circles under your eyes, then go for it. Wait. Look at who I'm talking to. You just flashed the entire construction crew and Palace. Oh, come on, that was funny and you know it. Ann, are you okay?"

"Huh? Yes, I'm sorry. I was daydreaming, but I don't have time for that."

Karen gives a small wave as she collects my wet, nasty clothes. I can feel her eyes watching me with concern, and I know this conversation will be picked up later over midnight snacks and a dirty movie.

"Is King Christian ready to see me?"

Tim staples a stack of papers. "Yes, Lady Ann."

We walk in and I nearly stumble as I see Mary sitting inside. I arch a brow at Christian. He smiles at me as he waves a hand to the chair next to Mary. "Have a seat, please, Lady Ann. Thank you, Tim."

"Good to see you, Lady Mary."

"You too, Lady Ann."

The tension between us is heavy as we turn our eyes to Christian. He clears his throat. "Thank you both for your hard work and dedication. I don't know how we would have pulled off the funeral and the coronation without your assistance."

He pauses.

"And now, I need you both to come together and help with another enormous event. I want you to plan the Christmas dance and dinner. Usually my mom handles this event, but she is beside herself at the moment."

"As you wish, King Christian, it'll be done." Mary nods. "After, of course, I return to the Palace with my family."

"I had forgotten about your trip to retrieve your family. When is that?"

"With your blessings, I leave tonight and I'll be back in a few days."

"You won't be able to accompany me to the library ribbon-cutting ceremony tomorrow morning?"

"If you want me to reschedule my trip, my King, you only need to ask."

"No, you should go visit with your family. I can take mom with me."

I bite my lip. "Christian, your mom has hardly left her room. Maybe a social event isn't a good idea right now. I have some free time tomorrow morning if you want me to go with you. You know how I feel about libraries."

I notice Mary purse her lips with annoyance. At this point, I'm not sure if it's because I never use titles with Christian, or the fact that she might miss out on a televised event.

"That's a wonderful suggestion, Ann. You can meet me downstairs after breakfast, and I'll inform your maid on what you should wear for the event. I don't want you to flash anymore unsuspecting people, especially since there will be children present."

I cringe as I see Mary's eyes widen. Whoops. I guess she didn't hear about my little water mess earlier.

"Thank you both again, for your support. I'm glad to see that the Christmas preparations are in good hands." He waves his hand towards his door.

Mary walks out without a backward glance, and I allow her to get ahead of me, not wanting to feel her icy glare on my back. I watch her walk to Ryan's room and knock lightly. Then the door closes behind her.

When did they become friends?

Back to the Basics

"I don't understand why I have to wear all of this."

I fidget with the ridiculous diamond tiara on my head.

"Ann, please stop touching your tiara. You might scratch a diamond."

"Like that would be the end of the world." I roll my eyes. "And it's not mine."

"We've been over this already. I gave it to you as a gift and it's yours from this day forward."

I narrow my eyes as I place my hands on it. "So that means I can take it off."

"For the love of—please, somebody, hand this woman her coffee before I throw her over my knee." Christian glances at one of his guards.

I'm rewarded with a large thermos of my favorite coffee and a basket of raspberry scones. I remove my hands off my tiara and I bite into the warm freshly baked pastry. I savor it as I watch Christian's exasperated face.

I love making him mad. In fact, it makes me happy to make him miserable. Especially when I haven't had enough coffee in my system.

After I am full, I offer him the remaining scones. He shakes his head and looks out the window with a distant expression. A car horn blares at a red light, but he doesn't bat a lash.

"If it would make you feel better you can take me over your knee." I tap my shoulder against his.

The guards crack a smirk but quickly change back to their stoic faces.

When Christian doesn't take the bait, I know something is wrong.

"Earth to Christian. I just gave you permission to punish me."

"Huh? My apologies, I was rehearsing my speech in my head. What was it you said?"

I grab his notecards out of his hand and glance down. No wonder he had that lost look in his eyes.

"Christian, I had no idea the library was being named after your father."

He forces a smile and turns to watch the city buildings pass by, and silence fills the air.

I smooth out my cyan colored gown, not sure what to say. I try to remember the many people who offered me sympathy when mom died. What helped me the most?

I grasp his hand in mine and squeeze. He doesn't turn away from the window, but he squeezes back, and the tension ebbs around us.

Once we leave the vehicle there is a rush of activity surrounding us. We take pictures in front of the library, cut the bright red ribbon, and shake hands with the head librarian.

"I never realized how much work goes into these press events."

I massage my sore feet as we sit in the children's area of the library, taking a break from the paparazzi.

"Thank you for attending this event with me, Ann. You did a fantastic job with the whole thing."

"I didn't do much. I smiled pretty for all the cameras. That's it."

"Ann, that means more than you know. It reminds the public of our country's strength and unity. And most importantly, it shows we care for the little things."

"Like public libraries."

"Yes, exactly right. Libraries are important for our future generation's education and imagination."

I turn as a group of thirty kids rush in... and towards Christian. I squeak as they embrace me and trample him.

Christian laughs as he lands on his butt and is surrounded by seven-year-olds. He waves his guards away as he sits cross-legged on the floor.

A red-haired boy plucks Christian's crown off his head and struts around with his chest puffed out like a rooster.

"Look at me. I'm the King. You must listen to all my rules."

I throw my hand over my lips to suppress my laughter.

Christian pulls the child into his arms.

"What is your first order of business, O' wise king?"

"Everybody gets to stay up super-duper late. Oh, and they can have all the donuts they want."

Christian glances at the librarian.

"Well, you heard the king, Ms. Stewart, donuts for everybody."

Boxes of donuts flock in. The kids squeal with delight as they grab handfuls of the sticky circles.

I offer Christian a hand up but he pulls me down.

"Trust my advice on this one, Ann. Once the sugar sets in, you'll want to be on level ground." He chuckles.

I sit crisscross next to him. I watch his eyes sparkle and it makes me smile.

17

"I didn't realize you liked kids."

"That is an absurd remark, Ann. Why wouldn't I like children? I told you I wanted a wife to bare me some of my own."

We are interrupted with wild chants demanding that Christian read them a story.

"What story shall I read, Lady Ann?"

I hand him over a classic and grin, as Christian glances over the title.

"You want me to read *Beauty and the Beast*?"

"What do you think kids?" I smirk at the group.

A blonde girl giggles. "King Christian is the perfect beast, and Lady Ann is the best beauty."

Christian wrinkles his nose but flips through the pages. I lean back with three kids in my lap as we listen. I laugh as he makes growling noises for the beast and high-pitched damsel in distress voices for Belle.

The kids clap and Christian bows at his audience.

"Lady Ann, my mommy says you are a farmer—is that true?"

I nod as I stroke her auburn hair.

"That's why she couldn't be picked for Queen," a frisky, dark-haired boy retorts. "Right, King Christian? Lady Mary was more pretty and smarter."

The boy's words sting. I wonder who his parents are, to have filled his head with such nonsense. I would love to find out and give them a piece of my mind.

"That's absolutely not true. Lady Ann was a wonderful choice for Queen." He offers me a smile. "How about I tell you one more story before you leave the library? A story about how Lady Ann rescued the Palace chickens from certain death."

Everybody leans in as he retells my tale. Bless him. He tries to make me sound heroic, but I'm not sure he meets his goal.

"Thank you again, King Christian and Lady Ann, for coming to the ceremony. It means a lot that you both took time out of your busy schedules."

"It was our pleasure, Ms. Stewart. I always adore the colorful rewards the children draw as a thank you."

"Yes, they do enjoy making paintings for you, my King. It's the highlight of their trip."

"I can already see the beast paintings now. You with horns and a hairy face will make this trip worth every second." I grin up at Christian's pursed lips.

The librarian coughs a laugh. "Lady Ann, you're always the charmer."

"I believe it's one of my most qualifying qualities of being a Lady." I elbow Christian. "Although most people don't appreciate my sense of humor."

"Well, we're always looking for qualified individuals at our libraries. And coincidently, we have an opening at Jessica's Memorial Library near your residence. If my memories serve me right, you spent many hours in that library."

My eyes twinkle at the name. "Yes, I have many fond memories of that place."

"Here's my card. Call me when you are in town and we can set something up."

Once we are back in the car, I release a sigh of relief and let my body sink into the plush seats. I'd gladly take a quiet field over a packed social event. Why anybody would want to be surrounded by people all the time is beside me.

I pluck the tiara off my head and let my hair fall loose around my shoulders.

"Ann, may I ask your opinion on a matter of importance?"

I turn my gaze from the window to his downcast face.

"Of course you can, Christian."

"Do you think I'll make a decent father?"

"Why would you even question that. You were amazing with those kids."

"Ann, you of all people, know what a monster I am." His eyes glaze over as he looks at my neck. "I hurt you in a moment of weakness. What if I do that to my child?"

"Christian, we all do things we regret. And you are working on your mental health, right? Doing your therapy sessions every other week. That says something. If you didn't want to change, you would never have sought out a professional. Remember it's progress over perfection. That's what you need to focus on."

"I'll never forgive myself for the anguish I caused you, Ann. I hope, in time, I can regain your camaraderie."

Christian turns to look out his window. I watch as the sun sparkles in his hair. Maybe choosing *Beauty and the Beast* was a bad idea for a book. But I didn't know he had all of this internal turmoil raging inside him. He is always well composed and stoic. This was a new view of Christian.

Once we return, I make my way over to Ryan's room.

The butler answers with a smile. "Lady Ann, it's lovely to see you again. Please, come in."

Ryan stands there with a light blue button-up shirt on, his hands in his pant pockets. He watches me, his dark eyes glittering. My heart melts as my own eyes scan over him. Since the day we met, I always thought he was handsome. Then as I got to know him, I appreciated his intelligence and empathy.

"Nice to see you, Ann." He opens his arms wide and we embrace in a warm hug.

The distance between us has grown since his father's death. I squeeze my arms around him and breathe deeply. I wish I could go back in time. I know I need to be patient—grief affects everybody differently.

"What's going on with you and Mary? I saw her come in here last night."

"Ann, are you spying on me?"

"Yes, you caught me, Ryan. Between all of my assigned tasks that have been donned on me, I spy on you with those few minutes I have."

"Mary came to ask me for shopping advice. Her parents are avid art collectors, and she wanted to bring them a present during her visit, so I made some suggestions. Are you okay, Ann?"

"Yes. I thought for a second you and Mary may have been meeting secretly."

"I wouldn't do that to Christian. Not that he would show me the same respect," he scoffs. "Or you. I see the way you act around Christian. But it doesn't matter because if we are both honest with each other, we have no chemistry."

My mouth falls open—where the hell did this come from?

"What did you just say? First off, you should know me better than that. And second, what do you mean we have no chemistry?"

Why was he pushing me away? After everything we have been through, I wasn't giving up without a fight.

"Ryan, if you think we don't have chemistry, let me prove to you that you are wrong."

"Ann, I love being your friend, and a part of your crazy farm life. Speaking of farm life, I checked out the coop today. It looks great. Your team is accomplishing a great task… and ahead of schedule."

"Very nice transition, Ryan. I'll let it go for now, but this conversation is far from over." Then I roll my eyes. "Thank you. We have been working hard. How are you healing? Didn't you have your stitches taken out recently?" I point to his stomach where he has a scar from his appendix removal.

He lifts his shirt to reveal tan abs and a scar, completely healed. I run my hand over it, remembering how scared I was of losing him. "It looks good."

As the words leave my mouth, the door opens and Christian walks in holding an envelope. He glances up as he shuts the door and drops the papers.

Ryan lowers his shirt. "Hey, Christian. What do you have for me?"

I stand straight, watching the emotions flash through Christian's icy eyes.

"I found those passport papers you were asking about for your trip."

I turn to Ryan. "You're going on a trip?"

Ryan shrugs. "After the holidays, I'm going to do some traveling and study new techniques for my artwork."

"So that's why you dumped me, you jerk. You want to be free when you travel."

"Yes, a near death experience has made me want to be with tons of exotic women, so I dumped you. Even though we never went out to begin with."

"Ryan, that's a little harsh. We may not have been officially going steady but we did have something. Plus, it was minor surgery, you were never going to die."

"Ann, please don't be angry," Ryan pleads at my retreating back. "I can kiss you as much as you need to convince you otherwise."

I raise my chin up. "I don't need your pity kisses."

Once I'm in the quiet hallway, I let out a sigh. I lean against the wall, taking in deep breaths. I was disappointed that Ryan thought we had no chemistry, but my feelings were more hurt that he was planning on leaving soon with no return date.

Christian walks out of Ryan's room before turning towards his own, running into me in the process.

"Oh, sorry, I didn't see you there. What are you doing standing out here?"

"I'm not sure, honestly. I ask that same question every day."

He places his hands on my shoulders. "I just begged you to stay here and help me. Trust me, you belong more than you know. How about we go to your room? I have a gift for you. I've been waiting weeks for it to be ready, and I'm excited to see how you react."

I smile, seeing the affection and admiration behind his eyes. I look down at the engagement ring on my finger. Was I going to keep this on? A constant reminder of the past.

"Christian, what you said earlier, about me still wearing the ring." I pull it off and hand it to him.

"Ann, we have been through this. You don't give back gifts, it's extremely distasteful. I understand if you don't want to wear it, but don't give it back to me." He runs a warm hand down my arm. "Ann, I wish I could give you what you are searching for, but I can't."

"Thank you, Christian. A lot has happened in a short amount of time and we both need to move on." I pocket the ring and force a smile. "Lead the way to this other gift, my King."

I look around my well-lit bedroom, but I don't see anything different from this morning. My eyes rest on a small kennel in the corner of the room by the window with a white sheet over it. I look over at Christian, who is smirking. I take a hesitant step in the direction of the cage and remove the draped fabric.

Inside sits a white fluffball of a chicken. It was a Chinese Silkie. I squeal with delight. My dad never bought show birds. He believed that chickens had to have a purpose and were not just for show or colored eggs. Kneeling, I open the cage door. As it swings forward, the little chicken struts to me, her eyes scanning her surroundings. I collect her in my arms and squeeze. Grinning ear to ear, I turn to Christian.

"Christian, she is so precious. Thank you."

He extends a hand to touch her. "I'm surprised you aren't trying to throw her back at me, like you tried to do with my other gifts. I'm delighted that you like her, Ann. She's specifically bred to be a house pet, so don't let her outside alone and while she is inside, make sure she wears her cover."

I arch a brow. "Christian, are you telling me that you, the King of the castle, are allowing a pet chicken in the Palace?"

He stands straight. "Keep her safe in your room, Ann. Unless, of course, you walk her outside on her lead." He clears his throat. "Although I enjoy seeing her, I better not see her walking the Palace freely, or she'll be rehomed immediately."

I stroke the hen softly, as tears brim. "Thank you again for another considerate gift."

"I hope you don't mind, but I named her for you — Snowball."

"Snowball seems like a fitting name for her."

"My attention is required in the office but I'll see you tonight at dinner."

Karen looks towards the door as he leaves. Then she turns to me. "What was that?"

"I don't know what you mean."

She laughs. "When is Christian going to leave Lady Mary and acknowledge that he's head over heels for you?"

"Karen, did you fall and hit your head? Please don't talk like that. Mary is a brilliant woman and Christian is trying really hard to make their relationship work."

"Somebody is moody. All right. I'm changing the subject now. Are you ready to see how to diaper Snowball?"

We both kneel on the plush carpet as we pull Snowball out. Karen holds her and pulls the diaper over Snowball's head, then under her wings and butt. We laugh until we cry as the white ball of fluff parades around with a flashy, red diaper. I wipe my tears and grab the lead. My eyes scan the little, metal tag that reads 'Snowball' on it. I even notice a small container of treats for her. I grab the container and shake it. Snowball's head pops up from across the room and she runs over, wings spread out, as Karen and I start laughing again.

I pull the ring out of my pocket and run it between my thumb and pointer finger. "Christian told me he can't give me what I want. I'm sorry that I was short with you, but the subject is uncomfortable at the moment." I hand the ring to her and look away as my eyes glimmer.

I stroke Snowball as she settles on my lap.

I squeeze my eyes shut as memories of my last conversation with Ryan resurface. "And Ryan said he'll be leaving at the beginning of the year to travel. He also informed me that he thinks we have no chemistry."

"Ann, you have had a rough day. How about I start a bath for you?"

"I appreciate it, Karen, but I think I'm going to get some air with Snowball. You know, test out the lead. Why don't you spend time with your husband?"

She goes to my dresser and places my ring safely in my jewelry box. She instructs me on how to put the lead on and gives me a rundown of the supplies for Snowball.

"Next, we need to make her some clothes."

We both giggle at the idea as we watch Snowball eagerly await her walk. It felt great to laugh again. So many serious events have happened that it was suffocating. Now here I am getting ready to walk my new pet chicken outside.

"Ready to go, Snowball?"

There wasn't much of a response. I pick her up and walk to the door. Karen follows us out and we both descend the stairs together. At the ground floor, Karen strokes Snowball and then departs to see her husband Vinny. I shudder at the memory of him being stabbed defending me against the former King's guard, Derek. It was a relief when Christian informed me that Derek was no longer here. I didn't ask for details, but I suspect he is somewhere in the ground. Exactly where he belongs.

Once we get out of the Palace doors and onto the soft grass, Snowball shakes and fluffs out her feathers. Then she struts a few feet and pauses to peck for bugs. We walk around the flower garden together and she scratches at the ground while I smell the beautiful roses.

I turn as I hear footsteps coming from behind me.

"Lady Ann."

I let out a breath as I recognize the voice. "Hey, Dan." I cock a brow. "I thought you went home for the day?"

Dan runs a hand through his short hair as he lets out a laugh. "It seems my job is never done." He stops short as he looks down at Snowball. "Did you get a new friend?"

"This is Snowball, my new pet chicken."

Dan kneels and focuses his emerald eyes. He stretches his hand down and strokes her. "Lucky little hen. Living in the Palace."

I sit in the grass and enjoy the warm setting sun with wisps of a cool breeze.

"I appreciate the bonus you gave my guys, but it wasn't necessary."

"Dan, I have all that I need right now. They have families to feed." I shrug. "It's my money and I can do what I want with it."

"I didn't mean to offend you, Lady Ann. It was very thoughtful." He rubs the back of his neck and lowers his eyes. "Compassionate as always. You are constantly thinking of others first." Then he looks back into my eyes.

"The world can use more compassion."

He nods and looks back down to Snowball. "So why the name Snowball? Why not Whitey? Or Blizzard?"

"King Christian named her for me. It was a gift from him and the name seemed to fit her, so I allowed it."

"I see. And how is his Highness and Lady Mary?"

"As strong as ever, of course. The King is still mourning the loss of his father but very capable."

"Of course, I wouldn't expect anything less from him." He clears his throat. "So, what do you do for fun around here?"

"Uh, well—nothing really. I work mostly. Is cooking fun? I do love to cook with the kitchen staff."

"Cooking? That's it? You should go to the city and explore. Have you visited the town yet?"

"No, I haven't had a lot of free time after the King passed."

He frowns. "Surely, you must be curious? I mean you have lived here for almost a year."

"Dan. I am a country girl, a home body. I don't mind staying at home with my chickens and friends."

"You are not just a country girl..." His eyes twinkle. "You help run one—an entire country, that is. Don't you want to view it and see how your work is affecting others?"

"I answer the phone and direct people on who to talk to in the office. That isn't much help, Dan. Although

I am curious about the country, I'm in no hurry to travel."

"Ann, you are rebuilding the Palace's chicken coop and teaching them how to free-range. That's definitely more than just answering phones. I understand you are in no rush, but I am planning on running into the city tonight to try a new coffee house the guys have been raving about. Would you be interested in accompanying me?"

"I don't think that's a good idea, Dan." My face gets hot.

"It's just coffee, Lady Ann."

I look down at my bare finger, where my ring use to be.

"I would love to have coffee with you, Dan."

He stands and brushes his pants off. "Great. I'll go clean up and then you can meet me out front."

I write a note for Karen, explaining that I am skipping dinner and going to get coffee with Dan. I glance down at the cell phone Christian gave me for work. I grab it and put it in a pink clutch purse with my wallet.

"I will be back soon, Snowball." I blow her a kiss.

She tilts her head before going back to pecking her food. I feel bad for locking her up, but I don't trust her wandering the room with no supervision. I descend the stairs with a pep in my step, excited to see the outside world after being cooped up for so long. The guards open the front door for me, and I step out into the crisp night air. I breathe deeply and feel the tension leave my body as I let the air out.

I spot Dan in a white pickup truck. When I walk towards it, he steps out and opens the door for me.

"I'm glad you decided to join me, Lady Ann." Dan smiles as he pulls out of the Palace gates.

"Thank you for inviting me, Dan. Would you do me a favor?"

He steals a glance at me. "Sure."

"While we are beyond the palace walls, could you please call me Ann?"

He laughs lightly. "You don't want your fans to recognize you?"

"I hate using titles. I'm just a regular person like anybody else."

"No problem, Ann. You know…" He taps the steering wheel. "We actually knew each other when we were younger. Before AnnaBelle passed away."

My mouth falls open. "Before my mom died."

"My family lived close by. We shared some classes in elementary school." He steals a glance at my blank face. "My dad helped repair your barn when that storm ripped through."

"I'm sorry, Dan. My memories before mom died are hard to recall."

I glance his way and stare at his silhouette. "Maybe my dad will remember better?" I laugh and shake my head. "He has a great memory."

"Jack's a good man, Ann. When my dad died, he helped me get over my loss. Then when I was starting my contracting business, he gave me contacts."

I look out my window at all the shops. The city was bigger than what I expected. I am amazed at how many people are out walking around. Soon we pull into a small parking lot outside of Becky's Cafe. I smile at the cute name as Dan parks and comes around to open my door for me.

"Thank you, Dan. This place looks great—it's small yet charming."

"Let's hope the coffee is good."

A little bell rings above our head, welcoming us. The nutty smell of freshly ground coffee assaults my nose. I look around the mocha-colored café with coffee art adorning the walls. Whoever owned this shop went to great lengths to make it feel warm and friendly. As we near the register, I glance at the display case with danishes, cookies, scones, muffins, and breads.

"Welcome to Becky's Café, how may I assist you?" the blonde barista asks us from behind the counter.

Dan waves me forward to order first. "Can I please have a Mocha Frappuccino, no whip, and a lemon pound cake." She types in the order and grabs my lemon cake and hands it to me. "Can I have a name for the drink?"

"Of course, it's Ann."

Barely finished scribbling down the letter "A", the girl's hand stills and she raises her head. Her eyes focus on my face. "Like *the* Ann? Lady Ann from the Palace?"

"Yes—"

"Oh my gosh! I cannot believe I am making your coffee. This is unbelievable—the girls will be so jealous. You must sign something for me. Or wait, better yet, can we get a picture together?"

I blink. "Can I have my coffee first?"

She lets out a laugh and nods, finishing up my name on the coffee cup. She writes 'The Lady Ann' on it. Dan orders a black coffee and blueberry muffin for himself with far less drama.

"I must be fifty shades of red."

He stifles a laugh. "It's better than fifty shades of grey. You're a little rosy, but you have to get used to this, Ann. You are in the public eye a lot, especially with everything going on."

"This is why I don't get out much." I poke at my lemon pound cake.

"Ann, is there really a problem with people liking you? You're kind, compassionate, and honest. People crave that in their government leaders. It's a breath of fresh air from, well, the old King."

I frown, not wanting to think about him. The barista comes up with our order and a menu.

"Here you guys go. Could you sign the menu for me, Lady Ann? The owner will be thrilled to hang it on the wall."

"Of course." I look down at her name tag. "Bailie."

Bailie grabs her phone while I sign the menu. "Say espresso." And clicks a picture of us. "Thank you!" Then she departs behind the counter with her treasures.

I sip my strong coffee and hum softly. "This is very tasty." I take another bite of my pound cake. "I wonder if Jock can make this for me?"

"Is Jock a friend?"

"Jock is the head chef in the Palace." I look around and lean in, whispering, "I sneak into the kitchen and help him cook and taste test new recipes."

I notice more people filing in. "Do you think we could take a walk outside?"

We sneak out the side door before anyone can notice me. Once we get back out on the sidewalk, I sigh. "Thank you."

"No problem, Ann." He watches me as I fiddle with my straw. "Is everything okay?"

"I guess I never thought I would be so popular." I kick a small grey pebble.

"The news had you pegged as Christian's favorite in the beginning. Then, Ryan's rebound once Christian chose Mary. Whether you like it or not, you are in the public's eye a lot."

My head shoots up.

"What about my important work at the Palace? Helping with the chicken coop, the funeral, the coronation."

"I didn't mean to hurt your feelings, Ann. I was just stating a fact."

I clutch my coffee. "I'm more than just some… some… heartthrob!" I retort.

He laughs at my red face. "Trust me, I know that from experience. I've been working side by side with you. You know your stuff and you are a hard worker, who isn't afraid to get your hands dirty."

I place my hand on his.

"Thanks, Dan, I needed to hear that. So, our project is almost done. Any ideas on where you're going next?"

I stop to glance into the window of Charles' Book Emporium. Their holiday display of books and knick-knacks is impressive. My eyes sparkle as I watch a bright red train weave around a stack of books.

"Well, Ann, there aren't many construction jobs around the city right now, so I'm not sure where I'll go next."

"I'm sorry, Dan. I can keep my ears open and make some phone calls on your behalf. Maybe there will be some work close by."

"That would be great, thank you."

We finish our coffees and toss them in a nearby trash can in front of Bernal Kitties and More. I press my face to the window as three black and white kittens play with an automatic mouse toy. Their collars jingle as they chase after it. Dan stands next to me and taps the glass gently. One kitten tilts its head towards us and saunters over with a soft mew. We giggle as the cat rubs its head against the glass.

My purse starts clucking. I look down at it, confused. Then I remember the cell phone hidden inside.

"Ann, where the hell are you?" Christian blares.

"Christian, I'm with Dan in the city."

"You're with the construction worker?"

"He's actually the contractor, Christian." I rub my temples, not wanting to ruin this moment with Christian and his jealousy.

"You're all alone with some guy that we hardly know. Why didn't you bring a guard with you?"

"Because I'm not one of your prisoners. I'm allowed to travel outside of your walls without your explicit permission." I sigh. "Christian, I'll be back at the Palace soon. Would you like me to bring you home anything?"

"Just you," he mumbles into the mouthpiece before hanging up.

As I place my phone back, I glance up at Dan. I never thought about how much I didn't know about him… before going out alone with him. Darn you, Christian, for making me paranoid of everybody.

I also didn't realize how popular I had become. A guard wouldn't have been a bad idea. I could have brought along Karen and Vinny.

"Sorry about that, Dan. King Christian thought it was a bad idea to leave without a guard."

"I'm sorry I got you in trouble, Ann." We start walking back towards his truck. "You guys aren't, I mean to say, you're single, right?"

"Yes, I'm single, Dan. Although I never asked my dad's permission to date." I smirk up at him. "I'm pretty confident I am old enough."

"King Christian just seems so protective of you all the time. That's why I ask."

I let out a breath. "Dan, rest assured, Christian and I are friends, and he is only looking out for my well-being."

Dan parks the truck inside the Palace gates and turns to me. "Ann, thank you for having coffee with me."

"Thank you for inviting me. It was nice getting out for a little bit."

"Could we try it again? Maybe try a dinner? I mean with a guard, if necessary?"

"My life is far too complicated, Dan. I think coffee was good, but I have too much baggage."

"I knew about your baggage and still asked you out."

"Dan, it's not worth it. I'm not worth it."

He reaches, grabbing my hand and bringing it to his lips before kissing it. "I think you underestimate your worth."

I feel a tingle run up my arm. I glance at my hand, then him. I bite my lip. "Ask me another time, Dan. I'd hate to get you entangled in my mess of a life right now."

"I'll keep asking until you say yes again."

Apologies

As I climb the Palace stairs, the warmth of Dan's words fills my heart. But the feeling is short lived as I turn the corner and falter at Christian's stern expression. I bite back my sarcastic retort—the one in which I remind him that he is not my daddy—and skip to an apology... to keep our conversation as short as possible.

"I'm sorry, Christian. Next time I go out, I'll bring a guard with me."

When I open my door, Snowball makes a clucking sound as she greets me. I smile at the warm welcome and watch as she explores the room.

Christian is right in front of me, blue eyes burning. I can feel the heat radiating off his chest. Oh, boy, he was fuming.

His eyes soften, as he rubs a hand down my face. "You frightened me tonight, Ann. I had no idea where you were or who you were with. I had to ask your maid where to find you... I don't want anything to happen to you."

"Don't be silly. I'm just a helper, Christian, and easy to replace." I joke, trying to lighten the mood.

Christian's eyes blaze. "Never say that again, Ann. I don't know what I'd do if anything happened to you. Promise me you will stay here and be safe."

I cock a brow. "What do you mean stay here? It's a little crowded here. Don't you think?" I push him away from me and sit on the edge of my bed to yank off my shoes.

"What's that supposed to mean?"

"It means I'm tired of being the third wheel and being known as the rebound."

"Who's saying those cruel words?" He balls his fists as he hears the pain etched in every syllable.

"Apparently everybody outside the Palace walls."

"Ann, I'm sorry, but you know that's not accurate. You're a vital part of this monarchy."

Snowball hops on the bed and sits in my lap. I smile and stroke her feathers. "I promise I'll be more careful next time I go out."

"What do you mean next time? Are you going to go out with him again?"

At his stern tone, I send daggers his way. He needed to remember his place. I won't let him control my life.

"Please, take a guard or invite him inside the Palace to spend time with you. There's an abundance to do here."

I roll my eyes. "Of course, my King."

He narrows his eyes and leaves as Karen steps inside. Once she shuts the door, she turns to me and purrs, "So, you and Dan went out?"

I fall back on the bed, making Snowball push out a startled squawk. "Sorry, Snowball."

"The guards just switched rotations and were talking all about it." Karen elbows me.

"We had coffee and took a walk together." I sit up and look at her. "I can't give him any more than that. I'm a mess, Karen. I mean I still feel like there may be hope for Ryan and me." I sigh. "It's hard to let go and move on."

I lean my head on her shoulder as memories of Ryan and me make my heart ache. Recollections of our spaghetti fight, him falling into the pond while trying to take my picture, and his beautiful memorial that he painted for Pecker.

I jiggle the jar Ryan made me and watch Pecker's feathers soar freely, before settling. Has grief twisted and blackened his heart? Could I pull him out of this funk before it was too late and I lost him forever?

I force the emotions down my throat before clearing it.

"So, Karen, how's Vinny doing?"

"Vinny is feeling better, and he's back in our room on light duty. I was going to go bring him some food. Do you want to visit with him?"

"That's a wonderful idea. It'll pull me out of my pity party."

"Hey, Karen, do you have any idea when my dad will be here? When we talked last, he was very secretive."

"Well, the maids have his room ready, but I'm not entirely sure when he is arriving. Sorry, Ann. I know you are eager to see him."

As we descend the stairs, Ryan comes up behind us and whispers in my ear, "Where are we going?"

I jump. "Nowhere with you."

"Ouch. Lady Ann, that's harsh. Aren't we BFFs? I thought you forgave me?"

We reach the landing, and he stops in front of me. I cross my arms over my chest, my hazel eyes narrowing.

"Which part did I forgive you for, Prince Ryan? The fact that you're abandoning me and going to travel the world? Or the fact that you told me you had no chemistry with me after leading me on?"

He blushes as servants side glance us. "Ann, come on. We have been through a lot. Can't we just be friends and be happy like we used to be?" He collects my hands

44

and uses his puppy-dog eyes on me, pulling at my heart strings.

I guess knowing that he feels we have no chemistry would make a friendship with him easier. Plus, I miss his dumb jokes and relaxed demeanor. My eyes wander over his body from under my lashes. I love how the light is dancing behind his pleading eyes. It brings me back to when he drove me to the farm and slept in the bed with me, while I cried myself to sleep because of a hen that had to be put down. Then the image of him in overalls flashes across my eyes. Then one of him covered in spaghetti. No matter what mess I was in, he was always there to help me out of it.

"Okay, we can *try* and be friends again."

He locks arms with me. "Wonderful, now where are we going?"

"We're visiting Karen's husband—Vinny."

"Oh. The guard that was stabbed? I've been visiting with him in the hospital wing. He's a great guy."

We walk to Vinny's room and peek our heads inside.

"Come on in, everyone. The food just arrived."

The kitchen staff sent over a wide array of finger foods. I am reminded of how little I have consumed today as my stomach growls angrily. We all take our fill of crab cakes, cream puffs, and tea sandwiches then

Vinny wraps an arm around Karen and kisses her forehead.

"I'm so happy you are out of the hospital, Vinny. And although I appreciate you saving my life, please don't jump in front of another knife for me. You scared us."

"You know me. I can't ignore a damsel in distress." Vinny chuckles then nods towards Ryan. "How's the trip preparation going?"

Ryan smiles. "Good. I have the entire excursion all mapped out. Three months of travelling, studying, and relaxing."

"I wish I could go with you, man." Vinny sighs.

Ryan tilts his head. "With all the extra money that the King gave you to keep quiet about the stabbing, I'm surprised you and Karen don't join in. Or at least have a sunny honeymoon."

Vinny laughs with Karen, grabs her hand, and rubs it gently. They both look at each other, nod, and then turn to me.

"Actually, we found the perfect item to purchase with that money," Karen says, beaming. "We're going to buy a home in the country and raise our child."

"Child?" I stutter.

Ryan shakes Vinny's hand and slaps him on his back. "Congratulations, you two. This is amazing news."

I'm still in shock as Karen comes over and grabs my hand. "Yes, child." Then she places my hand on her belly. "I've been wanting to tell you, but we wanted to do it together."

I hug her tightly. "I'm going to be the best aunt. Just you wait and see."

It was nice to be around friends and relax again. To embrace life's tiny treasures. A child is one of the greatest gifts that life can offer, and I couldn't be happier. They've helped me in many ways, and I hope I can repay them by being there for them and their child.

Ryan wraps an arm around my waist as I swipe at my wet cheek.

"Can I be an uncle?"

"Absolutely, Ryan," Karen says before she smiles at Vinny. Then she elbows me. "Do you want to know where we'll be living?"

"Are you moving closer to your parents?"

"Oh, goodness no. I couldn't live any closer to them, they would absolutely suffocate me. Actually, your dad helped us find land to build on, a few miles from yours. Apparently, someone was downsizing their property and your dad put in a good word for us. Our new home should be ready before the baby comes."

My dad never mentioned any of this to me when we talked on the phone. The biggest news he shared with me was that him and Suzie had parted as friends. He didn't give me any details, and before he asked me to drop the subject, he said they're on good terms after their breakup.

"That's wonderful, Karen. I can't wait to help you set up the nursery and get the house ready."

They both look at each other, then to Ryan, who shakes his head. I tilt my head and look up at him. "They're trying to ruin the Christmas present I have for you."

Before I can squeeze any more information out of them, they flip the conversation to potential boy and girl names, infant clothes, baby equipment, and everything baby.

My head spins at all the research Karen has done on infant care. Who knew that babies needed all kinds of special gear? I bite the inside of my cheek as she continues to swipe through her gift registry.

When Karen's fingertip hovers over a labor and delivery website I switch topics and converse about house plans.

"Do you guys need a contractor to help build your dream home?"

"We have a contractor already, why?" Karen asks.

"Well, the coop will be done soon, and Dan needs a new project for him and his guys, or they'll be jobless afterwards."

Karen frowns. "That's not good. I know Dan is a hard worker. I'll ask around for him."

Vinny settles under the navy comforter, his eyes closing. Karen kisses Vinny's forehead and then he places a kiss on her belly.

Ryan's fingertips graze my elbow and I get the hint.

"Well, we'll let you guys get some rest." I walk over for one more hug. "Sleep well."

Ryan and I slip out and close the door behind us.

"I can't believe they'll be leaving the Palace and having a child soon."

"You didn't expect them to live here and serve forever, did you?"

"I guess not." I rub my arms to cover the fib. "But what'll they do now?"

"Employees of the Palace have no problem finding employment after they leave. I'm sure they'll find work easy and if not, I'll put in a good reference wherever they want to go."

"I'm going to miss them."

He quirks a brow. "Aren't you planning on returning home after the chicken coop is done?"

49

As we get to my room, I stop. "I never thought about it, honestly. I've been here for so long helping Christian. I just assumed I would stay for as long as he needs me."

"But what do you want, Ann?"

"I don't know. I'm flying by the seat of my pants. Taking it day to day."

He gestures with his hand to my pictures hanging on my wall. I love taking photos of nature, family, and most of all chickens. And my favorites always ended up on display.

"I think you do know what you want, Ann. You're just too afraid to ask for it."

He wraps me in a hug. "It doesn't have to be tonight, but maybe have a goal by the New Year?" He kisses the top of my head. "Ann, I'm sorry that I pulled away from you when my dad died."

"Ryan, don't be sorry. When mom died, I distanced myself from my friends until I didn't have any left. I felt like it was easier to lose them sooner rather than later… or suddenly." I look around my room. "Actually, coming to the Palace has been great for me. I made new friends and let them in without the fear of losing them."

"I'm grateful you came to the Palace too, Ann."

He pulls back and smirks at Snowball. "So, this is Snowball?"

She pecks at the ground, then settles on my bed. We both stroke her, stuck in our own thoughts. My hand flies to my lips as I suppress a yawn and Ryan smiles. "That's my cue to get out of here. I'll see you tomorrow." Then he grins at me. "Once your surprise arrives."

"What surprise? You've been talking to my dad, haven't you? When is he coming? Is it tomorrow?"

He shrugs, laughter brightening his eyes.

"Why is it he tells you, but not me?"

"Because he loves me more, apparently," he teases, reminding me of the bond him and my dad built.

I grab a pillow and toss it at him as he closes the door.

I lean back into my bed and hold Snowball close. It felt good to laugh with Ryan again. I bite back tears as I try to imagine a world without him in it.

Maybe I was wrong— I *am* worried about losing those I love.

Time Marches On

The sky is clear, and the sun is shining. I'm in a lush field with red, sweet-smelling flowers laughing and chasing a little girl as she pursues a black hen. When I catch up to her, I lift her up and swing her around. We both fall to the grass, breathless.

I move slowly when the sun beams in my face, demanding I begin my day. I open my eyes and stretch my stiff muscles. As I sit up, I blink down at my outfit. I was so exhausted last night, I never turned off the lights or even changed my clothes.

I turn and see Snowball happily pecking her water. She pauses as she looks up at me and chirps. I bend down and offer her some freeze-dried mealworms. Christian would have a canary if he knew I let her roam free all night.

"Were you a good girl last night?" I glance around "No accidents or messes?"

After inspecting the room, I release a sigh of relief and I change into some tight-fitting jeans and a red tee shirt before heading to breakfast. When I get there, I see three new faces surrounding Mary and Christian.

"Lady Ann, allow me to introduce you to my family. This is my father Governor Patrick, my mother Nicole, and my brother Max."

I shake hands with them as Mary proudly points each of them out to me.

"It's a pleasure to meet you all. I'm sure you must be very proud of your daughter and her many accomplishments here at the Palace."

I spot Ryan a few seats away from the happy couple.

"If you'll excuse me."

"Good morning, Mr. Sunshine."

"Is it? I hardly slept. My dreams were ruined by crying babies and nagging women," he mumbles as he rubs his temples.

"Sounds to me like someone is afraid of commitment," I tease as the butler pours liquid gold into our mugs.

"Please don't say the C word so early in the morning."

"Ryan, one day you'll meet a woman who is perfect for you. And the C word won't be so intimidating."

In the corner of my eye, I see my dad poke his head into the dining room.

"Dad!" I run to him and squeeze him tight.

"Ann! I missed you so much. Look who I found on my way up here."

Elizabeth is pale with large dark circles under her eyes. "I saw your poor father looking around here lost, while I was on my way to breakfast. He was so kind I assumed that he belonged to you." She smiles up at my dad, who offers her one in return.

"Thank you, Elizabeth. That was very kind of you."

Elizabeth sits between Ryan and my dad. I cock a brow at Ryan, who shrugs and watches his mom.

"Christian, this is my father Jack."

Once they're done shaking hands, he turns to his mom.

"Mother, would you like to sit next to me and meet Mary's family?"

"I'm not feeling up to it right now, sweetie. Maybe after we eat, dear."

Christian's smile falters and a heavy blanket of tension falls over the room. Everybody side glances Elizabeth.

Once Christian returns to his seat, she shrugs. "I'd rather be in the company of people who don't expect me to be cheerful and put together." She glances towards my dad. "You've survived great loss and you understand what I'm trying to say." She dabs her eyes with her napkin.

I pat her hand and meet her gaze. "You're an adult. You can do what you please. Plus, you are still

Christian's mother. So, feel free to put him over your knee to punish him."

It has been a while since I have seen her smile. I glance towards my dad, then back at her, and realize that Elizabeth is right. They're both widows, survivors. They have a lot in common. The food arrives and we all dig in, except for Elizabeth.

"Maybe you should try some oatmeal or grits? They would be lighter on your stomach," my dad eases out.

She pushes her plate away. "That is a wonderful idea. Thank you, Jack."

"No problem. Grief is hard. But you're missing out on these eggs. They're delicious."

Soon there is small talk about the food and coffee. Then Ryan and dad discuss plans to add an office to our barn. Somebody clears their throat, and we look up to see Christian.

"Mom, are you ready to meet Mary's family?"

Christian walks Elizabeth over. Afterwards, I see her and Mary talking. All of a sudden, Elizabeth's face turns red and she starts yelling.

"Of course not! Christmas has been planned and executed by me for decades!"

Mary's glances towards Christian, her expression pleading for assistance.

"Mom, we just thought that with the recent events, you would need some more time off."

Elizabeth's jaw clenches. "My husband died. But I'm still very much alive and able to perform the duties expected of me." She raises her trembling chin and stomps off.

Dad scoots his chair out and moves to Christian. Christian frowns and pats my dad on the shoulder. Then my dad walks back over to us.

"Ann, honey, I'm going to try to see if I can talk to Elizabeth."

I turn to Ryan. "What just happened?"

Ryan leans back, watching my dad follow Elizabeth. "My guess is your dad is trying to share his wisdom with mom." He shakes his head. "He is one brave man. My mother is a ball of nerves right now."

"My dad was too, when mom died. It was months of this. At least until he joined a support group. Then it got better."

I sip my coffee, trying not to enjoy Mary's ruffled feathers as she slowly sits back down. In the corner of my eye, I see a white blur pass by the open door.

"Did you see that, Ryan?"

"Huh? See what, Ann?"

I squint and squeal, causing everybody to glance my way. Christian looks at the empty doorway then back to me.

"What's going on, Ann?"

"Oh, nothing."

I dazzle him with my widest smile as I move towards the doorway. I peek around the corner and I know I am in big trouble.

"That had better not be Snowball falling down the stairs, Ann."

I jump, realizing that Christian is right behind me, when he hisses in my ear. I force out a playful giggle as I push him back towards Mary's family.

"Don't you worry about a thing, King Christian. Go and spend some time with your soon-to-be in-laws."

"Ann…" He begins to threaten.

"Oh my, I'm sorry my dad's calling my name. I'll catch up with you guys later. It was so great meeting you all."

Before he can lecture me, I dash down the stairs three at a time. Crap, Christian is never going to let me live this down.

"Snowball?"

I peek inside the many open doors, with no luck. My eyes fall on the worst possible room for her to be in and I swallow.

"Snowball, are you in here?"

I gasp and charge after a bald man as he holds Snowball over a pot of boiling water.

"Let her go!"

The man stops and turns to me.

"Lady Ann?"

"Put her down, this instant."

The man looks down at Snowball and then the pot of water.

"I wasn't going to cook her. I was just…"

I snatch Snowball from his hands and glare.

"What's with all the commotion in here?"

The head chef Jock turns the corner and grins at me.

"Lady Ann! It is so nice to see you again. Oh, and you brought a friend?"

"Well, actually she somehow escaped my room and made her way down here. Then I saw baldy over there, trying to throw her in to boiling water."

"Sir, I wasn't going to cook her. I was holding her while I checked on the water for the pasta."

"Dale, why don't you go sanitize the counters for me."

Dale grumbles but walks away.

"Yeah, that's right, Mr. Clean. And if I see you around my chicken again, I'll have Jock give you a magic eraser and throw you on toilet duty."

"It's always a pleasure seeing you, Lady Ann. Your aura brightens my day." Jock smirks as he stirs the pasta.

"Thank you, Jock. I should get her back upstairs, before the King decides she is better suited for the table than as my pet."

I sneak up stairs and make it to my room just in time.

"Ann, I need to have a word with you."

Oh crap! I fling Snowball in my room and turn to face Christian.

"Christian, shouldn't you be with Mary and her family?"

"Where is your chicken, Ann?"

"In my room where she belongs, of course. Where else would she be?"

My angelic smile does nothing for his sour mood.

"Listen to me, Ann, while Governor Patrick and his family are here, there will be no more escapes. Do you understand me?"

"Does that mean after they leave, she *can* escape?"

My joke does not sit well with him. He narrows his eyes and holds his hands up in mock defeat.

"My King, you have my word that Snowball will be on her best behavior from now on. Cross my heart and hope to fly."

"Christian? There you are. I have been looking for you. My father would like a tour of the grounds. And since it is such a lovely day, I thought we could all go together." Mary loops her arm around Christian.

Before Christian can continue his barrage, I slide into my room. I let out a breath as I wipe my forehead.

That was close.

I blink at Karen as she changes Snowball's diaper. "Getting some diapering practice in, Karen?"

"If I can diaper a chicken, I can diaper anything."

Ryan rushes in. "Can I hide in here with you ladies for a minute? Mary is trying to persuade me to walk the property with her and her family." He grins down at Karen. "Nice job!" He walks to Snowball, freshly diapered, and strokes her. "It looks like Snowball is settling in well here. I'm glad you like her."

"Did you help Christian pick her out for me, Ryan?"

He blushes. "Well, when I visited your house, I read in your chicken magazine about a breeder that specialized in domestically-trained chickens. Then when Christian wanted to give you a special gift for all of your help, I suggested this."

I watch as the chicken walks around looking for stray treats. "Ryan, did you help Christian pick out my ring too?"

"Maybe a little."

I groan and fall back on my bed. "I gave him all the credit." I grab a pillow and throw it at him. "Why didn't you say anything?"

He pulls at the corner of the pillowcase. "I'm used to being in the shadows and helping others while not getting the credit. I'm okay with that."

"Ryan, that's not fair. Next time you have a hand in any of my gifts, please allow me to give you the proper credit. What you helped to create was beautiful. Thank you."

We hear the door open and we all turn to see my dad. With a smile, he pulls something out of his pocket. Ryan eyes his car keys, and he jumps up to retrieve them.

"I followed the Palace driver here in your car. I didn't think you would mind."

"Thanks, Jack."

My dad looks down at Snowball. "I can't believe you have an indoor chicken with a diaper on. You know how ridiculous that is, right?"

"You're just jealous, dad."

He stands with Snowball in his arms. "She's a sweet little thing. Could I borrow her?"

"Do you want to take her for a walk?"

He shakes his head. "No, I want to see if she can bring a smile to Elizabeth. May I?"

I hand him her lead and treats. "Can I come too?"

"Of course, Elizabeth has nothing to say but good things about you, Ann. And who wouldn't?"

Adrie opens the door and smiles as she lets us in. I look around the large suite. The last time I was in here, it was so dark and gloomy. Now the curtains are drawn, and Elizabeth is at her writing desk taking notes.

"Come on in, everybody. I apologize for my outburst this morning."

"It's all right, no need to apologize. We understand."

Elizabeth's eyes light up at the sight of Snowball. "What's that?"

My dad walks Snowball over to Elizabeth and smiles. "This is Ann's little chicken. I thought you may want to meet her."

Elizabeth looks up at my dad, then to me. Then she reaches out to touch Snowball but before she can, Snowball jumps onto her lap.

"She's beautiful, Ann. Her feathers remind me of cotton candy."

Ryan steps forward and scans Elizabeth's notebook.

"Are you sure you're up to organizing the ball this year, mom?"

"Ryan, honey, this is my last year doing it. Lady Mary will take over next year."

We all turn as Christian comes in, staring wide-eyed at the chicken in his mom's lap. He quirks a brow but doesn't ask.

"I'm glad everybody is here. Mary and I would like you all to join us in the ballroom for a quick announcement."

Our eyes fall on Elizabeth. "As you wish, Christian." She hands the chicken to my dad. "We'll be right back, Jack. Hold onto her for me."

As we enter, I see Mary smiling and standing by her family. As Christian enters, she beams and grabs his hands. They both look towards the small crowd, and Christian speaks up.

"We've agreed that with Mary's family here, we want to have our wedding as soon as possible."

Elizabeth clears her throat. "Christian, how soon is as soon as possible?"

"Next month," Mary says, smiling up at Christian.

My jaw drops and the reaction is the same on everyone, but it's Elizabeth who speaks first.

"That's really soon. Are you sure you'll have enough time to plan a wedding of this magnitude?"

"I've been planning my wedding since I was a little girl. And even more so now, because I knew it was going to happen sooner rather than later. I only have to get all the details set in stone. And with you taking on the ball, I have some free time on my hands."

I feel the blood drain from my face. Why did it hurt so much? I thought I was past this. Christian and Mary are perfect for each other. Both are selfish and pompous know-it-alls. I swipe at my eyes before anyone can see them shimmering.

Warm fingertips tickle my arm. I steal a quick glance and see Ryan standing next to me. I grab his hand like it's a lifeline, willing his strength to keep me on my feet as my world spins out of control.

I reach the gardens and gasp for air. I bring my knees up to my chest as I sit by the little pond, in the shade of a towering oak tree. Silent tears fall, splashing into the stagnant pool as images of Christian, holding me in his strong arms while laughing, start to take shape—I shake my head, resolving to never cry over Christian again.

He has chosen, and I will respect his choice and move on.

The peaceful surroundings dim, as I hear footsteps approaching my sanctuary. Quiet and lost in his own thoughts, Ryan sits next to me. We sit there watching the fish swim around. I lean my head on his shoulder and find comfort in his silent presence.

My lips pull back as I remember the last time we were here. I had brought my camera to take pictures, and he ended up taking it from me and falling into the water. I giggle at the memory.

"What are you thinking about over there, Ann?"

"Do you recall the last time we were here together?"

The pond glimmers off his dark eyes. "They were simpler times, weren't they?"

"Maybe for you, but I was constantly watching my back and trying not to get sent home."

He arches a brow at me. "You are joking, right? You never cared about being sent home. It seemed like you were begging to go back."

"You're right I did, at the time anyway."

He wraps an arm around my neck and pulls me close. The physical contact reminds me of the day he told me he loved me.

For a moment, I feel that connection of understanding as we're lost in each other's gaze. Then he turns towards the fishpond.

"Ann, do you love Christian?"

"To be honest, I'm not sure what that kind of love feels like. I've never had a serious relationship before. I mean, I know the love my dad and I share. But that's it. I have strong feelings for Christian, but I do for you as well."

I pull away from him and wrap my arms around myself.

He taps his shoulder against mine. "You know you never said I love you back to me when I was in the hospital."

I look up at him, his eyes searching mine. I fight the urge to move a lock of loose brown hair from his forehead. "You were on heavy medication, Ryan." I look away. "And you never said it again after that night. Plus, I'm not sure what love is."

He sighs as he watches the colorful fish swim around. "Who's the one person you see spending the rest of your life with? Someone you could tell anything to and do anything with. When you see them, you smile from ear to ear and you look forward to seeing them again when they're away from you."

"Listen, I'm sorry for bringing it up." He rubs his stubble. "It's been a chaotic few weeks. And now we'll be planning a wedding and Christmas. This trip can't come soon enough."

I clear my throat, trying not to think about Ryan leaving me too.

"I should go check on Dan and the crew before it gets too late."

He tilts his head as he glances towards the pen. "Ann, are you and Dan dating?"

"Ryan, I'm not looking for a relationship right now. Men are too complicated, and it hurts too much when they decide they don't want to be with you anymore." I elbow him.

His lips pull down as my words echo around us. "Not all men are complicated, Ann." He shrugs. "But you know, women may be better for you anyway." He winks at me.

"You need to get that picture out of your head, right now."

I walk towards the coop, feeling his watchful eyes on my departing figure.

As I get closer to Dan, he looks up and waves.

"Hey, Lady Ann, it's good to see you again. Are you coming to check on our progress?" He removes his bright hard hat, wipes his brow, and then replaces it.

"Yes, I am and it looks great. How are we tracking on our timeline?"

"Not too bad. At this pace, we should be done before Christmas."

We walk around the yard, glancing at the progress on the pen walls. Then we walk around to the coop, as the roofers hammer away at the shingles.

"I haven't forgotten about you guys. I'm still looking into getting some projects for you after this job is complete."

"I appreciate that, Ann. Actually, King Christian asked us to help build a few things for the wedding and found us a job about a day's drive from here."

"That's great… that he was able to get you work." I rub the back of my neck.

"I had a feeling that it was to keep me away from you." His lips quirk. "But then I found out about Lady Mary, and his wedding too, so maybe I misjudged his intentions."

We stand there in the afternoon sun, watching the men hard at work. It feels good, making progress when my life feels as though it is stuck in neutral.

All of a sudden, I hear a loud bang coming from above us. I watch as a hammer topples over, ready to fall off the roof. I gasp as I notice that the trajectory is right over Dan. I shove him and get us both out of harm's way.

Something hard hits the back of my head and I feel blinding pain. Then everything goes black.

Mending

I groan as the smells of rubbing alcohol and latex gloves assault my nose. I feel a pair of warm hands on my arm and I hear far off mumbling, but it's hard to make out. I try to open my eyes, but they are so heavy. I drift back into the blackness.

The next time I come to, everything is blurry and out of focus, but within a few seconds it clears. Out of the corner of my eye, I see Ryan standing over me, watching my every move. In one of the padded chairs against the wall, I see my dad wringing his hands together.

"Where the hell am I?" I croak.

"Ann, just lay back. You're in the hospital wing. A hammer fell on your head."

"Ugh, it feels like a house crushed me. My whole body hurts."

I lean back against the pillows and Ryan pats my hand. "I'm going to get the doctor. I'll be right back."

"Dad, I'm so sorry I worried you and ruined your vacation. I should've been wearing a hard hat. I am such an idiot."

"You're all right and that's all that matters." Tears brim his eyes as he kisses my hand.

70

The doctor comes in, followed by Ryan. After he's done looking over my wound, he turns to Ryan and my dad.

"We'll keep her overnight for routine observation, but I think she'll be all right. Apart from a bump and a few staples on her head."

I reach back and touch my scalp, but cringe at the sudden movement.

"You need to move nice and slow, Lady Ann," the doctor says. "I'm going to get some food for you and see if you can hold it down."

"Is there any way I can recover in my room?"

"Let's see how you do with some food and a good night's rest. Then maybe you can go to your room in the morning."

"Dad, you look exhausted. Why don't you go check on Snowball for me?"

"I'll come back after I grab a bite to eat." He kisses my forehead, pats Ryan on the shoulder, and walks out.

"My dad looks like he has been sitting here for days. He looks so burnt out. Are you okay, Ryan?"

"A hammer falls on your head, and you're asking if I'm okay? You are some woman, Ann."

"How bad is it, Ryan?"

71

He swallows. "I am walking back from the pond and all of a sudden, Dan is yelling for help. I rush over and I see you on the ground covered in crimson." He shakes his head. "I thought you were gone."

I see a tear forming and I reach a hand towards him. He grabs my palm and rubs his face on it.

"I meant how bad is my wound," I tease.

He laughs. "Well, unfortunately, you have a bald spot where they had to clean and staple it."

"What? You said I have a bald spot? Great, just in time for the wedding." I roll my eyes.

The door swings open and Christian rushes in. "Oh my God, Ann. They just told me you were awake. How are you feeling?"

I rub my face and look into his bloodshot eyes. "Apparently, a hammer landed on my head. How do you think I feel? But dad and Ryan have been keeping me company."

Christian looks at Ryan. "I'm grateful they can be here for you too. Did the doctors say if you'll be released soon?"

"Yes, they did."

"Good, we have much to discuss when you return. Now get some rest and get well soon. That's an order."

I lean against my soft pillows, feeling sleep pull me back into its void.

"Don't worry, Ann, I'll be here when you wake up."

"Don't be silly, Ryan. Go and get some rest in your bedroom."

He scoots next to me and his warmth lulls me into a restful sleep.

When I wake up, I'm surprised to be surrounded with flowers, balloons, a plush chicken, chocolates, and fruit baskets. I look next to me and I don't see Ryan. Wondering where he went, I lean towards the door where there's a small strip of glass. Outside my room, I see him talking with the doctor.

I lift my hand to the back of my head and touch the cold metal of the staples. I wince as a pain shoots through me. Lured by their enticing aroma, I lean forward and reach for one of the bright red strawberries, tucked away in an adjacent fruit basket.

Ryan comes back in, eyeing my mouth around the large strawberry. "Are you hungry?"

"This fruit basket was conveniently placed within reach." I smirk at him. "Who brought all of these gifts?"

"Everyone sent you goodies—Christian, Karen, your dad, my mom, and Dan. But don't fill up on fruit, the doctor is coming in with a nurse to help you stand. Then we can get you some heartier food."

He sits on the edge of my bed and plucks a green apple out of the basket.

"What were you and the doctor talking about out there? Is he concerned with my progress?"

"He mentioned that sometimes people with head injuries can be unstable afterwards. Sometimes permanently or just temporarily."

"Well, we both know I've been mentally unstable for a while."

He shakes his head and chuckles, as the doctor comes in with the nurse. "Good morning, Lady Ann. How are you feeling today?"

"I'm hungry and eager to get back to my room and see my chicken."

The doctor glances at Ryan.

"King Christian bought Lady Ann a pet chicken and it lives in her room."

The doctor lets a breath out. "Well, once we get these assessments done, you can do just that, young lady. I'm going to start with some questions. Answer them the best that you can."

He reads from a list of questions, testing basic knowledge, short-term memory, long-term memory, and routine habits.

All of these questions make my head throb.

"That went well, Lady Ann, you've passed with flying colors. Now for the hard part."

Ryan bends down to kiss my hair. "I'll be right outside if you need me." Then he disappears behind the door as the nurse moves a curtain and comes over to my bedside.

I look towards the nurse then the doctor, who smiles. "We are going to try to get you to stand and walk over to the bathroom on your own. But we are here to assist you if you need it."

I take a deep breath and throw my legs over the side of the bed. Then I lower one at a time, until my bare feet touch the floor. I shiver as the cold creeps up my thighs. This flimsy gown offers little warmth.

"Are you okay, Lady Ann?" The doctor's gaze assesses me.

"Just peachy, doc."

I wobble for a minute, but take baby steps towards the bathroom. I make it there, but my head is pounding. I slump against the door frame and wipe the dampness off my forehead.

"Please take your time, Lady Ann," the doctor warns.

One step at a time, I make it into the bathroom.

When I stand back up, my legs are too shaky, and the nurse helps me back to my bed. The mixture of cool air against my already sweat-covered body forces a shiver down my spine. I plop down on the mattress with a sigh as I tuck my toes under the warm covers.

"Well done, Lady Ann. Why don't we get you some food? Then you can build up your energy. That way you can return to your room."

"Could I have something for this headache too, please?"

He nods, before opening the door and giving Ryan his conclusion. Ryan reenters the room, frowning as his eyes sweep over me.

"Please don't look at me like that. I'm not as frail as you think I am."

He grabs a moistened rag and sits down on the bed. His strong hand pats my forehead gently. Then he scoots closer and lets me borrow his warmth. As I listen to his steady heartbeat, I feel myself start to drift off to sleep. But the ache is too great and I can't achieve it.

The doctor comes back in with a tray of food and several pills.

"Try to eat some soup, Ann. Then you can take your medication. And if you can hold that down, I think it'll be safe for you to go back to your room."

I force my eyes open and as they focus, I quirk a brow at the spoon in Ryan's hand.

"I'm not a baby, Ryan. I don't need to be fed."

My words sting and he pulls the spoon away.

"I'm trying to help in any way that I can, Ann. I feel so powerless."

I watch him for a minute, remembering how helpless I felt when he was in the hospital getting his appendix removed. I sip the tasty chicken noodle soup from his spoon, and a smile spreads over Ryan's face. Greedily, I slurp the salty soup and devour the buttery dinner roll. Then I take the medication with some water.

Ryan moves my hair off my forehead, and I peek out, watching him. I smile as he catches my eyes. My world spins as the medication courses through my body. I run my hand down his rough stubble.

"You need to shave and take care of yourself, Ryan."

He shakes his head and sits next to me. "I'll rest when you're safe in your room."

"I love you, Ryan."

I'm not sure what his response is, but I drift into a deep painless sleep, happy to have such an amazing friend by my side and looking out for me.

When I wake up, I hear voices and feel my warmth gone. I rub my eyes and see the doctor, Christian, and Ryan talking. I stretch carefully and yawn.

"Don't let me interrupt you. Carry on, boys." I flutter my hand at them.

Christian rolls his eyes. "Well, she seems to be back to her normal sarcastic self." He grabs my hand and strokes it. "Ann, you really frightened me when you were brought into the hospital. I almost had Dan killed on the spot," he teases.

"Hmph. I see my sarcasm is rubbing off on you. And my world class eye roll. It wasn't his fault I got hurt. I should've been wearing a hard hat."

"I'm grateful that you're feeling better." He opens his mouth then closes it. Patting my hand, he smiles, and walks to the threshold. "I'll see you and Ryan soon."

"I think you're ready to return to your room. But if you need me or if anything changes, call me," the doctor concludes before exiting.

Ryan reaches for my hand. "Did you mean what you said last night?"

"Well, you do fit the requirements. You're someone I see spending the rest of my life with. I can tell you anything and do anything with you. When I see you, I smile ear to ear, and I look forward to seeing you again when you're gone." I shrug. "But I know it's complicated between us. I mean, you said we don't have chemistry. Plus, you're my closest and dearest friend and I don't want to lose you."

He bends down and places a kiss on my cheek, inches away from my lips. I let out a soft moan. But I choke on it. Not a *friendly* kiss on the cheek. I see the smokey look in his eyes, and I know mine reflect the same, and yet I'm still in the friend zone.

The nurse interrupts our staring contest as she rolls in a wheelchair. She pushes it to the edge of my bed, and she and Ryan help me down. I sit as the nurse places a soft yellow blanket over my lap. Then Ryan steers me towards the elevator.

"Ann! I'm so glad to see you!" Karen squeezes the breath out of me.

Ryan collects me in his arms and places me under the soft floral comforter.

"I missed you too, Karen. Ah, this bed is so much better."

There is a soft knock, and the smell of food wafts in. My eyes light up as I spot a grilled cheese sandwich and French onion soup.

Before I touch the food, I narrow my eyes at Ryan.

"A deal is a deal, mister. I'm safe in my room, now get some rest. And please, for the love of God, take a shower. I'll be fine. See, no hammers in sight."

He leans his forehead on mine. "I almost lost you, Ann."

My heart skips a beat as I consider his words. "You'll always be a part of my life, Ryan. We have a little niece or nephew to help raise."

"Can I come back to check on you later?"

"Of course, you can."

His hand hovers over the doorknob, then he turns to me, his dark eyes sparkling. "I love you too, Ann."

Once the door clicks, Karen squeals. "I knew it! That man has had a crush on you since you arrived here! It shouldn't have taken another life crisis for him to see that."

"Calm down, Karen. He also said we have no chemistry. And I understand I'm not Dr. Love, but I know that's important in a relationship."

"Oh, well, maybe we can change his mind with a little coercion." She grins.

I eye the food tray as the aroma beckons me. The French onion soup warms me to my toes. And the grilled cheese melts in my mouth.

"Karen, can you grab me some comfortable clothes to wear, like my favorite chicken pajamas? And help me to the bathroom?"

I take my time and make it to the bathroom with a lot less assistance than last time. Karen helps me into my soft pajamas, and I lean on the door frame, unsure if I can make it to the bed.

I glance at Karen's pregnant belly and bite my lip. I didn't want to put extra strain on her.

There's a knock on the door, and I hear somebody enter. Christian strides over with Mary at his side. I feel Mary's eyes sweep over my chicken pajamas.

I bite the inside of my cheek at her polished arched brow.

"My King, my Lady, to what do I owe this unexpected visit?"

Christian walks towards me with an outstretched hand. "Ann, let me help you to the bed. You look like you are about to faint."

I swat his hand away. "I'm fine. I'm just taking a breather and enjoying the—uh, view."

He quirks a brow. "The view, huh? And what exactly are you viewing, Ann?"

Another knock, and Ryan walks over, his hair wet and face smooth.

He tilts his head at me. "Ann, what happened?"

"Ann is enjoying the view apparently," Christian says, rolling his eyes. "I offered her my assistance, but she is being stubborn and declined."

Ryan chuckles. "Christian, you just need to learn how to properly deal with stubborn women."

Ryan scoops me up in his strong arms.

I squeal at the sudden motion. "Ryan, put me down this minute!" When he tightens his grip, I laugh and nuzzle into his neck, smelling his aftershave. "Ryan, I'm so glad you *finally* showered. How about we take this party to the balcony and get some fresh air?"

Ryan carries me out into the bright sunlight. The golden hues make my eyes water. I wipe the sweat off my brow and sigh, wishing I could gain strength quicker.

I hate feeling so helpless, especially in front of Miss Perfect Mary. Her baby blue sundress and silver-painted nails mock me.

Karen comes out with a pitcher of water.

"Should I get some refreshments, my King?"

"No, this won't take long."

Before Karen moves away, I pipe in, "Karen, that soup wasn't very filling. Would you see if Chef Jock can make a pizza for me?"

Mary wrinkles her nose at my food choice.

"I'll ask Chef Jock for you, Lady Ann."

I lean back, allowing the sun to soak into my skin. A warm breeze tosses my brown hair, and I wish my head wasn't throbbing so I can enjoy the warmer weather and take a stroll around the garden. I can smell the fragrant flowers from up here. They are teasing me.

My eyes flutter open and I see everyone staring at me. I force a smile and sit up to the best of my ability. "Go ahead, my King and Lady. I'm all ears."

Christian clears his throat and squirms in his chair before Mary grabs his hand.

"As you both know, our wedding is fast approaching." He pauses and looks towards Mary, who urges him on with a squeeze of her hand. "And after the wedding, the couple goes on a honeymoon."

Ryan and I look at each other with quirked brows. Why did Christian look uncomfortable talking about this?

"Mary would like to travel to her hometown for the honeymoon. So, we'll be out of reach and—busy."

Was Christian uneasy talking about being intimate with Mary? I cover up my snort with a fake cough and Ryan squeezes my leg.

"What we need from you two is to take Christian's place for a few days while we are away. You know, cover the basics for him in the office," Mary finishes for Christian.

Now, I am speechless. They want us to handle everything at the Palace. I look to Ryan and he seems surprised, but he recovers quickly. "Of course, Christian. Whatever you need from me."

Christian lets a breath out. "Thank you, Ryan. What about you, Ann? Do you think you'll be able to assist?"

"Of course, I can."

"Thank you."

Once Christian finishes his water, he stands and offers a hand to Mary, but she remains sitting.

"May I have a word with Lady Ann alone, please?"

Ryan looks towards me.

"I'll just be inside when you are done."

When the door closes behind them, I turn towards Mary. She places her hands flat on the table and then folds them together. Her blue eyes lock onto mine. "Lady Ann, what are your plans for Christmas? Will the chickens be settled in their new pen by then?" She tilts her head and blonde tendrils cascade over her shoulder.

"The coop was ahead of schedule before my accident, but I don't see why that would put them behind." I cross my arms over my chest. "Why don't you tell me what's on your mind and stop beating around the bush with your false pleasantries?"

Mary blinks at my forwardness. "To be honest with you, Lady Ann, I don't trust that Christian's completely over you and I don't feel comfortable with you living in the Palace."

"Lady Mary, I have no intention of having any kind of relationship with Christian, other than what's appropriate." I pinch the bridge of my nose. "If you're *really* that insecure, I can leave after you and Christian return from your honeymoon."

"Thank you for understanding, Lady Ann. Our marriage needs to be resilient enough to withstand the pressures of our people." She sighs and leans back. "Now that our business is taken care of, can you clarify a rumor for me?"

"What rumor?"

"That Prince Ryan and you are a couple."

"It's complicated and really none of your business."

"I'll get Ryan to help you up and back inside. Thank you again, Lady Ann."

I stick my tongue out as she passes. The nerve of that woman.

Christian and Mary are gone by the time Ryan brings me inside. The room feels cool and dark. Ryan lays me on the bed and brings the soft comforter to my chin.

"What was that all about?"

"I'm leaving after Mary and Christian get back from their honeymoon."

"What! Why? Did Mary threaten you?" Anger burns behind his eyes.

I snort. "Of course, she didn't. But she would like to start her new life with her husband without having his ex-girlfriend around."

"I see."

"It'll be better for everyone, Ryan. We can all move on with our lives."

He looks up at me with a frown.

"You may say you love me, Ryan, but without chemistry, how do you think we can have a relationship?" I run my hand down his face. "You deserve the whole package. Love and chemistry. And so do I."

Before he can respond, Karen strides inside with my pizza and my eyes grow wide at the glistening toppings.

Ryan laughs and pulls away. "I see where I rate." Then he winks and walks towards the exit. "Christian wants to teach me his special filing system in the office, but I'll check on you soon."

"You aren't going to share this pizza with me?" I shout as he closes the door.

Karen climbs into the bed next to me. "I'll share it with you. My feet are killing me and I'm starving!"

We eat the fully-loaded vegetable pizza in a comforting silence.

"Karen, where is Snowball and my dad?"

"Your dad took her and Elizabeth to that support group meeting. It's so sweet the way Snowball and Elizabeth get along. I saw her talking to the seamstress about making Snowball a snowsuit. Can you imagine that?"

"I'd hate to separate them, especially if Snowball is helping Elizabeth. I'll have to ask Elizabeth if she wants to keep Snowball when I leave the Palace." I take another slice as Karen watches me.

"When are you leaving, Ann?"

"Lady Mary asked me to leave after they come back from their honeymoon." I shrug. "Which is fine. I can get back home and return to farming with dad. Plus get ready to be the best aunt!" I rub her belly.

"Well, if that's the case, Vinny and I will prepare to leave soon... There's no point in staying here with her bossing everyone around."

"But will your house be built by then?"

"If it's not, your dad invited us to stay with you guys."

"That's the best idea he has ever had. I can already imagine our late-night movie nights and sugar-induced comas."

After we stop laughing, I sway from the pain in my head. Karen grabs a pill, settles me under the covers, and leaves a glass of water on my nightstand.

"I'm going to check on Vinny. I should be back before you wake up. If you need me before that, the phone's right here."

I shut my eyes as she switches off the lights on her way out. When I leave the Palace, I know I will miss the busy life, but I'm glad I can take my best friend along with me.

Mysterious

I grab the water off the nightstand just as the door opens, and I make out Ryan's silhouette. He turns on the lights, and I blink for a second to adjust.

"I checked on you earlier, but you were sound asleep. How are you—Ann, you're bleeding."

My hand goes up to my head and I feel wetness between my fingertips. "Did I pull a staple out?"

"It just looks bloody back there. I'll give the doctor a call and update him."

I hear Ryan explain the situation to the doctor before hanging up. "He said it's normal." He sits on the edge of my bed. "Do you want help cleaning up?"

"No. Thank you. Karen should be back soon, and I can only have sponge baths for a little bit because I can't get the staple area wet."

"Sponge baths, huh?"

I swat him and change the subject. "So, Karen and Vinny might return home with me. At least until their house is done."

Ryan smiles. "That'll be nice, having them close by." He wrings his hands then looks at me. "Ann, I don't want to ruin your Christmas surprise, but I'm anxious you'll make plans if I don't."

"Ryan, what are you talking about?"

"Remember when you found out that I was traveling after the holidays?"

"Of course, I do. I was disappointed that you were leaving."

"Well, there were two sets of papers."

I wait for him to continue but he just stares at me.

"You mean you're taking someone with you?"

He nods.

"Who are you bringing with you?"

He pulls a piece of paper out of his suit pocket and places it in my hand. My mouth falls open when I see my name and picture on it. "You want to take me? But—" I stammer.

"Christian and I thought it would be nice for you to see the world. You can take some photos, amplify your portfolio, and get a break."

"What about my dad and Karen?"

"It wouldn't be forever, just a few months. We'll be back in plenty of time for the baby. And your dad already gave me the thumbs up."

"So, you *have* been talking to my dad behind my back."

"What do you think, Ann? Do you want to travel the world with me?"

"I would be honored to tour the globe with you, Ryan. I hope my stamina will be up by then." I lean back.

"The doctor says it won't be a problem. The trip is still a few months away and we won't be doing anything strenuous."

"Are you sure you want to take me? I mean you can take anyone you want." I bite my lip. "You know, maybe someone you have chemistry with?"

"Ann, I shouldn't have explained the situation to you like that. At the time, I didn't know how to put into words how I was feeling." He sighs and watches me. "Of course, there's chemistry between us. But you and Christian had that, and Cherie and I had that too. And look what happened. I'm terrified of ruining our friendship, just like what happened with Cherie and me."

My heart breaks as I see the pain etched on his handsome face. All this time I assumed Ryan was dealing with grief and needed time to heal. But I was wrong. Cherie had damaged Ryan when she cheated on him. Now I need to help him pick up the pieces and put his heart back together.

"But there's hope for us, right? I mean, Christian and I seem to be doing rather well as friends."

"Do you *really* think you and Christian are doing well as friends, Ann? I mean you are doing so well that his fiancée's asking you to leave after they get married." He laughs at my blush and continues, "Christian still has feelings for you. Which is another reason why I backed off."

"I'd never do what Cherie did to you, Ryan. Surely, you know that, right?" I put my hand on his arm.

"You might not, but I'm not so sure about Christian."

I take in a breath. "Okay, let's be friends. I can wait. I've waited my whole life."

He runs his hand along my jawline, and I lean into his warmth. "Thank you for understanding. I know as hurt as I am over Cherie… you witnessing Christian getting married to Mary must not be easy. I'm here if you need someone to talk to."

A knock sounds on the door and Tim pops in. "Lady Ann and Prince Ryan, the King requests your presence in his office."

"Thank you, Tim. We'll be right there."

I slip my shoes on, pausing to call Karen and ask her to change the blood-stained bedding on her way up from Vinny's. I stand with Ryan's arm around my waist.

"You don't need to hold me, Ryan. I think I can manage to walk to the office."

"I know I don't *need* to, but I want to hold you."

I roll my eyes at the mixed messages he's sending me. It's exactly what Christian put me through.

I knock on the door and Christian answers immediately. He ushers us inside the office.

"Thank you both for coming so quickly. The results from dad's tissue and bloodwork have come back." We inch forward. Christian rubs his face and sighs. "It seems that everything's normal."

"That's good, right?" I glance from Christian to Ryan.

"It's odd that a man of good health and with no indication of heart disease falls dead one night," Ryan speaks out.

Christian leans back in his chair, and he stares at a spot on the wall while tapping a pen to his lips. "We'll still be diligent. I'm sure father has enemies because of his unique tendencies when dealing with individuals."

I scoff. "That's sugarcoating it, Christian. Your dad was a murderous liar."

Christian clears his throat. "Thank you both for coming. Please remember that I don't want this information to leave this room."

"Of course, we understand. Let me escort Ann back to her room, and then I can help you finish that financial report." Ryan stands.

"Thanks, Ryan, I appreciate all the help I can get. Maybe with your assistance, I can complete it before dinner time."

As we pass Elizabeth's room, my dad strides out laughing.

"Ann. It's great to see you out and about, sweetie." My dad embraces me gently.

"Thank you, dad. I'm feeling better than yesterday, but the healing process has been slow." I rub the back of my aching neck. "How was the support group meeting?"

My dad looks towards Elizabeth. "It went smoothly, and we hope to have a weekly gathering here at the Palace. Oh, and Snowball was an absolute hit. Everybody really connected with her."

"You know, Snowball will need someone to watch her while I heal. Then again when I go with Ryan on vacation." I look towards Elizabeth.

"I'd be more than happy to keep watch over her."

"And with all that time away from me, she may get attached to you. Would you consider adopting her if Christian is okay with it?"

She beams. "If you're sure you are okay parting with her. I'd love to adopt Snowball."

Karen's in my room changing the sheets and pillowcases when we enter. She smiles at us as she fluffs the pillows.

Ryan kisses my head. "I'm going to help Christian with that report, but I'll see you later at dinner."

When the door closes, I catch my dad watching me with a smile.

"What, dad? Do I have something on my shirt?"

"Don't you think for one second that your act of kindness went unnoticed, young lady. That was very generous of you, to allow Elizabeth to adopt Snowball." He sits next to me. "My little girl is growing up right before my eyes. Your mother would be so proud of all of your accomplishments."

I swipe at my cheek and clear my throat. "You know, we haven't spent much time together. How about you push me in my wheelchair, and we can get some fresh air?"

"That's a wonderful idea. I'd love to see your progress on the chicken coop."

After Karen helps me clean up, dad wheels me outside. I can smell the Fall foliage in the air and my heart aches to return home, to watch the leaves change and the chickens molting. I turn to my dad and see the same distant expression on his face.

"So, who's watching our feathered ladies while you're away?"

"Suzie's watching the chickens for us. Her family's flying in for the week and she wants to show the grandkids the chickens, so it's a fair trade."

"I'm glad you two are still friends. It would be awkward going home otherwise."

"Actually, I'm thinking about retiring and doing some traveling soon."

I laugh and shake my head. "What? You? Retire? That's a good one, dad. Coming from the man who's never traveled on vacation. The same man I've never seen in a bathing suit."

I swipe at the side of my eye, at the thought of my father in a Speedo.

"Ann, I'm serious. I've been restless lately. I want to travel for a while and put my skills to work helping those less fortunate. I have a few projects planned out… where I can help build homes for the homeless and be a support group leader to areas in need. I won't be too far from you, and I think it'll be exciting."

"Wow, you are serious. If that's what you really want, dad, I won't hold you back."

"I'm hoping Elizabeth will travel with me. She could use some time away from all of this."

"Really? You and Elizabeth, huh?"

"When you lose the person that you love the most in life. It's hard to move on. So, we have a mutual understanding—a bond between us."

As we get closer to the coop, dad pauses. "It's wonderful, Ann."

Dan looks up from his clipboard and jogs over. "Ann, it's great to see you out and about again. Did you get my gifts I sent you?"

His smile broadens as he looks up at my dad. "Wow. Mr. Jack. Long time, no see." They hug and laugh.

"Danny, you are looking well. It's been, what? Ten years?"

"Yeah, it's been a while." Dan rubs his pink neck.

All the construction workers come over to shake hands and offer their warm greetings. Soon everyone's chatting and enjoying each other's company.

After the sun dips down, Dan dismisses his crew for the evening. Then he offers my dad his personal cell number. Dan pats me on the leg and says goodbye before heading back to clean up.

My dad pushes me through the beautiful flower gardens, and I run my hand over the soft, fragrant petals. I let the birds' songs wash over me as I close my eyes and enjoy their symphony.

"I can see why you like it out here, Ann. I haven't seen so many different varieties of flowers in one place before now."

After strolling the grounds, dad pushes me back to the Palace. "Danny is a nice boy, isn't he? I had always hoped the two of you would have hung out together more. But I'm glad you have Ryan. You guys seem happy."

"Thanks, dad, but I'd rather keep you separate from my dating life."

He chuckles as he presses the button for the elevator. By the time I get to my room, I'm surprised at how much better I feel than I had earlier.

"It's nice to see some color back on your cheeks, Ann," Karen says as we enter.

"It was nice going outside and getting some fresh air. And I learned something new." I smirk at my dad. "My dad wanted me to date Dan."

My dad blushes as Karen suppresses a laugh. "All right, young lady. Stop making fun of me." He kisses my head. "I need to wash up for supper. I'll see you soon."

Karen chuckles as the door closes. "Dan isn't a bad person to end up with, Ann. He is charming, handsome, and great with his hands." She wiggles her digits for emphasis. "And your dad already approves of him too. Bonus."

"So, what am I wearing to dinner?"

"Fine. Keep your love life hidden from me, brat. But heed my warning, girl, I'll find out one way or another. How about a nice light dress and flats?"

"Karen, I have *no* love life. Get over it. Can't I wear jeans? I'm wounded after all. Certainly, Christian can make an exception to the dress code for me."

She tosses a baby blue dress at me. "Suck it up, buttercup, you aren't on vacation yet."

Karen pulls back my hair and applies light makeup. I smile in the mirror, glad to be able to stand on my own with minimal pain. Karen locks eyes with me in the mirror and I watch as she rubs her belly.

"I'm so happy for you and Vinny." I turn to her. "Thank you for all your help."

Karen blinks back tears. "Aw, thank you, Ann. I'm here for you anytime you need me. Even if you won't talk dirty with me."

We hug and my heart fills with happiness. I can't imagine my life without her.

When I open the door, I tilt my head as I see Ryan standing there, hand in mid-knock.

"Are you feeling better, Ann?"

Ryan's friendship was another relationship I was forever grateful for. My eyes travel over Ryan's body, and rest on his chiseled face. Feeling daring, I grab his bright red tie and pull him to me.

I brush my warm lips over his for a brief second.

When he stands straight, he blinks and offers his arm. I accept it and we walk to the dining room without another word.

I grin to myself, confident that we have chemistry, and that this relationship could blossom if we wanted it to, even with his reservations.

When we get there, the room is decorated with red and green streamers, mistletoe, and twinkling lights.

Ryan pulls out a chair near my dad for me.

"Ann, you look lovely this evening," Elizabeth comments.

"Thank you. The festive decorations are stunning."

Her icy eyes glitter as she assesses her handiwork. "Thank you. I'm glad that I got out of bed and did something, other than mope. It feels good to stay busy."

The atmosphere is filled with good spirits as the waiter brings out mixed drinks and stuffed mushroom appetizers. As I pop one into my mouth, I tilt my head to the soft background music of "O Holy Night."

Ryan turns from Christian. "Ann, you're looking a little pale. Do you want to go lie down?"

I try to turn my lips up as my vision blurs. "Maybe that'd be a good idea."

As Ryan buttons up his jacket and offers his arm, I feel everybody observing me. I hate this attention and the pity etched on their faces.

"Why don't you finish eating with your family, Ryan? I will bring Ann back to her room."

My dad offers an arm to me as Ryan promises to check on me later. As we go out, I let out a breath I didn't realize I was holding. I try to maintain a straight face through the dull pain.

I ease on to my bed as the room tilts. I watch my dad wring his hands and pace.

"Dad, are you all right?"

"Yes, of course. It's just that Elizabeth asked me to ask you to do her a favor. But I don't like the idea of getting you involved."

Karen sits next to me as she helps me get ready for bed.

"Elizabeth feels that Lady Mary's rushing into this wedding with King Christian. She also thinks Lady Mary may have hidden motives. Especially since she heard that Lady Mary asked you to leave."

I consider his words. "What could Lady Mary possibly be trying to accomplish with an early wedding, dad? I mean they were always planning on getting married, right? Why is the timing suddenly suspicious?"

In the corner, I see Karen squirm in her seat.

"I told Elizabeth the same thing, Ann. But sometimes when you lose someone so suddenly, you feel like you have to blame somebody for their death." He rubs his hand over his stubble.

"I can poke around and see what I can find out for her. You can tell her I will keep my ears open and report back if there is any news."

My dad kisses my forehead. "Don't worry about Elizabeth, sweetie. I'll take care of it, now get some rest, Ann. I'll see you in the morning. I love you."

"I love you too, dad."

I turn to Karen with an arched brow when the door clicks. She shakes her head. "Asking questions won't lead to a positive outcome, Ann."

"Karen, you need to tell me what you know about Lady Mary."

She sets her hand on mine. "It's not my place to tell you, Ann. You need to talk to Ryan."

My jaw drops. "You mean Ryan's involved with whatever's going on with Lady Mary?"

"You look like you are in a lot of pain. Let me grab your medication so you can sleep."

My world spins as I burrow under the covers, wanting them to bring warmth to the coldness that has crawled up my spine, at the possibility of Ryan betraying my trust.

Unwanted Answers

Yawning, I stretch my body out. As I step out of bed, I'm relieved when I don't feel the shooting pain in the back of my head. Turning, I see the sun shining brightly through the large windows. I walk out onto my balcony and look around at the crisp morning scene. The sun is painting a beautiful array of oranges and reds against the backdrop of the lush vegetation.

Enjoying the coolness of the quiet morning air, I see the nearly complete coop in the distance. A smile spreads across my face. I'm grateful for the opportunity Elizabeth has gifted me. She has always been kind, understanding, and supportive. I owe it to her to look into Mary's decision to rush the wedding.

"Good morning, Ann. I thought you may want breakfast brought up to you. How are you feeling?"

I look down at the large portion of bacon, eggs, sausage, and biscuits with a side of fresh coffee. "Thank you, Karen. I'm feeling a lot better today."

"You look healthier. There's a lot more color to your skin. Has Prince Ryan come in to check on you?"

Swallowing some eggs, I shake my head. "No, I was getting ready to throw some clothes on and hunt him down."

"I'm sure he's busy in the office with Christian."

I pull on a pair of blue jeans and a blue V-neck tee shirt. As I walk out the door, Karen stops me.

"Ann, please don't be mad at me for not telling you what I know about Mary."

"Although, I am not fond of the idea of you keeping secrets from me. I'm not angry with you, Karen. Because I know you have my best interests at heart."

She wraps her arms around me and squeezes.

"Let me know if you need anything else."

As I walk past Ryan's room, I hear Mary's voice behind his door. Why is she with Ryan? Curious, I open the door and peek inside.

My eyes grow wide as I see them sitting together, intimately. Mary's low-cut yellow sundress doesn't hide much as she stares up into Ryan's dark eyes. She places a polished hand on his.

"Ryan, please," she draws out.

He leans in towards her, lowering his face to hers. Their eyes turn to slits. My heart catches in my throat as I gasp for air.

Throwing open the door, I clench my fists. They both jump and look at me.

Mary opens her mouth, but then closes it. Ryan brushes past me and shuts the door before turning to my scowl.

"Ann, why don't you sit down?"

Taking a deep breath, I bring my hand across his cheek. "How dare you."

Mary gasps. "Lady Ann, I'm surprised at you. That's no way to treat Prince Ryan."

I take a step towards her, my hand itching to strike that perfect face.

Ryan grabs my arm as he rubs his other hand over the red patch of skin. "Ann. Please, calm down. This isn't what it looks like."

Narrowing my eyes, I pull my wrist away from him. "What the hell's going on in here?"

They both look at me. Then back at each other.

Ryan sighs, running his hands through his hair. "Please. Calm down, Ann."

"Tell me to calm down. One. More. Time," I hiss at him through my clenched jaw.

Mary shakes her head. "Not here, Ryan."

My eyes dart to Mary again. When did she stop using his title when she addressed him?

"How about we go for a walk, Ann?"

Ryan opens his door and pulls me out into the vacant hallway. Mary walks towards her room, while Ryan and I descend the stairs.

Once we are outside, I lower myself on a bench, and cross my arms. Even though the birds are singing, and butterflies are fluttering around us, my anger is making bile rise up and into the back of my throat.

"Why the hell were you two alone in your room like that?"

"I've never given you any reason to doubt me or my intentions. I've always been honest and open with you, Ann. You didn't have to slap me."

I scoff, "Except when you forgot to explain to me about your dad being controlling."

"But other than that?"

"Other than that enormous detail. You've been honest with me." I kick at a pebble. "But, Ryan, walking in and seeing you two that close is suspicious."

"Ann, Lady Mary was upset. We were talking and that's it."

"Ryan, Mary has a fiancé she can confide in! Remember, your brother? What do you think Christian would've done if he walked in and saw you two? There's something more you are not telling me. Why did Karen say I had to talk to you about Mary? What did she do?"

He looks down at his hands. "When my dad had Derek take you and lock you up, Christian was in the hospital wing with Vinny." Ryan rubs his cheek. "Well,

Lady Mary came to me and told me what happened to you and Vinny. I was still recovering from my surgery and I couldn't do much, but I knew time was limited. I knew my dad wasn't going to stop until he killed you and Vinny too, to cover up his tracks. I couldn't let that happen, Ann." His dark eyes bore into mine. "I had to do something, before it was too late." He watches my face, eyes brimming. "Mary had an idea. An idea I wasn't on board with at first." His words rush out. "But it would solve our problems and make sure no harm would come to anyone else by the hands of my dad."

My face pales. "Oh no." I release my words slowly. "Ryan? What was Mary's idea?"

"There's a rare, untraceable herb. If administered correctly, it can cause a person's heart to fail."

"What?" I squeak out. "Ryan, are you telling me you killed your own father?" I jump up, no longer able to be near him. I pace close by, pulling my hands through my hair. "How did you get this herb in time?"

Ryan stands and grabs my hands before I can run off, squeezing them until I meet his gaze. "Mary had the herb, and she had willing servants who made sure dad took it. Ann, please. It was to save your life."

His words slice daggers into my heart.

"Why would they help her? That was their King," I whisper.

"Ann, my dad has hurt many families in his time, and when he decided to mess with you, there were plenty of volunteers to help take him down. No one wanted to do this, but your life was in danger."

"So, they decided a life for a life. How's that fair? I never agreed to that."

"We knew you wouldn't agree. That's why you spent that night in the cell."

"This makes no sense, Ryan. How did Mary magically have this rare herb in her possession?"

"She was planning on using it to save her family from dad's threats, and when he grabbed you, she had the opening that she needed to put her plan into action."

"Why didn't Christian tell me about this?"

An uneasy silence blankets us.

"Because we never told Christian what happened."

My world spins and I brace myself against a tree. "Ryan, I can't believe you haven't told Christian any of this."

"I was hoping the autopsy would bring something to light. Then it could give me an opening to say something, but it didn't and now he's so busy with the wedding."

"We *need* to tell him."

Ryan's head shoots up. "He could have us sentenced to death."

"Not you, Ryan, because you were bedridden for God's sake. This is all Mary's fault."

"She was trying to save her family, and, in the process, save you. How can you not see this?"

"Ryan, your brother has a right to know what his fiancée schemed up, before he commits his life to her in marriage."

"I'm sorry. I won't do that to him." He glares down at me and as if by instinct, I flinch, noting how much he suddenly resembles his father. "And you can't say anything either."

"Are you threatening me, Ryan?"

"I have to protect my family from knowing this truth, Ann."

"I hate to ruin your grand master plan, but your mom's already suspicious of Mary."

"What do you mean? That's impossible. We have been very careful."

"Elizabeth asked me to keep tabs on Mary... because she is rushing the wedding with Christian. She asked me to let her know what Mary's up to."

"Then throw her off the trail, and tell her you found nothing wrong with Mary."

I glare at the stranger in front of me. "I'm not going to lie to her too. Absolutely not!"

"You obeyed Christian, when he asked you not to tell mom about the possibility of dad being poisoned. How is this any different? Ann, it's for her own good."

"That was different because your brother didn't have the evidence yet. You aren't concerned about these facts hurting anyone, you are nervous about being reprimanded for your actions."

I push past him, but he grabs my wrist and pulls. We glare at each other, and I start to see the resemblance between him and Christian as well—his unwavering stubbornness.

Why is it his job to protect his mother and brother? Why can't he just be honest and let Mary take the fall? Why is he trying to protect her too? Who's to say she won't do this again with Christian?

There must be consequences.

I pull my arm from Ryan's grasp and rub it.

"Please, Ann. Let's just forget about this and move on."

"Obviously, Mary can't move on if she's running to you in secret to discuss it. This is a mess, Ryan, and it complicates everything. Especially between us."

I stomp off, turning heads as I go. A wet drop lands on my arm and I reach up to touch my cheek.

Why was I always crying?

Once I am safe inside my room I start pacing in thought. This is insane! Ryan and Mary plotted and murdered the King.

I jump as somebody opens my door without a knock. I look up and see Mary and I send daggers in her direction.

"Lady Ann, may I come in?" she asks as she closes the door behind her.

"No, you need to turn around and get out, before I do something that we will both regret. I don't want you anywhere near me, you murdering fake."

I feel red hot heat rise to my face. I pin her against the wall with my body and glare into her icy eyes.

"I did it to save you." She blinks at my aggression.

"Do you think I am stupid? You're a liar. You never gave a chicken's rear end about me. You only wanted to save your family and you were willing to kill for it. Now get the hell out of my room."

"Shh!" She waves her hands.

"You should've let me die. I never wanted to exchange a life for a life."

"Lady Ann, Ryan loves you. He was the one that decided on the when. I just had the how." She squeezes past me. "The King kept dangling my family over my head. It was so nerve-racking. I just wanted them safe."

"Why didn't you tell Christian? You'll be his wife soon and you can't keep this secret from him, especially if you want a successful marriage."

"But what will he do to me and Ryan?" She looks up with pleading eyes.

Karen enters with my lunch and frowns at Mary, who wipes a few stray tears then walks out without a backward glance.

"Karen, how long have you known?"

"I overheard them discussing their plan of action and confronted them. They talked me into the idea by stating Vinny's life was in danger... because he knew too much." Her hand goes down to her belly. "I'm sorry, Ann. I wanted to tell you, but I knew how upset you would be. And it was already too late."

I poke at my chicken Cordon Bleu. "Everybody has lied to me."

"We were just trying to protect you."

"Well, I never asked you to. So now what? We all pretend like this never happened, and go on with our lives?"

I can't keep something like this from Christian or the Queen. I play with the idea of returning home early, and before the wedding.

I can blame my head injury and just leave and never come back, never see them again.

But am I a coward?

"A penny for your thoughts?" Karen pleads.

"I think it's time I return home and let everything go back to normal. The coop's almost done and with this head injury, I'm not sure how much help I can be for Christian anyway."

"Ann, are you sure?"

"But, hey. It'll give you a chance to settle in with me at the house, right?"

"You still want me around you, after hearing all that?"

"You're my best friend and you had nothing to do with this mess, other than knowing about it."

"Thank you, Ann." She embraces me.

There's a knock on the door.

"Ann, Tim's here and he says Christian's expecting you in his office."

I knock on Christian's office door and he gestures for me to come inside. I stop short as I stare down at Ryan. Ryan avoids my eyes as he looks towards Christian's desk.

"Ann, Ryan tells me you're returning home?"

My jaw drops. How did Ryan know? I just decided this and only told Karen.

"Yes, I'm considering it."

"He said you two are having relationship complications, and your head injury is taking longer to heal."

I clench my jaw at Ryan, who continues to find Christian's pen interesting.

"Yes, whatever Ryan said is true."

I storm past Tim and the other office workers, unable to be anywhere near that liar.

Karen's head turns as I walk in. "That was fast."

"Ryan has some nerve. He told Christian I was leaving and that he and I were having complications."

"Well, it's not a lie, sweetie."

"Yes, but I came to that conclusion on my own. I was deciding to leave. Ryan's trying to kick me out to save his butt," I hiss.

I turn to the open entryway and I'm surprised to see my dad. "Ann, honey, I heard you yelling, is everything okay?"

I pinch the bridge of my nose.

"Of course, dad, I just have a headache. I'll be fine."

"Why don't you take it easy and go to bed early? Here, I'll tuck you in."

I feel like I'm five years old again as he pulls the covers up to my chin and kisses my nose.

"Ann, I'm sorry I stressed you out with Elizabeth's request. Please don't worry about Lady Mary. I'll take care of it."

"Oh, dad, it wasn't you." I frown. "Ryan and I aren't seeing eye to eye at the moment."

"Well, don't you fret. Tomorrow is a brand-new opportunity to start fresh. Sleep well, Ann."

Karen sits on the edge of the bed. "Do you want me to stay with you? I can get some rocky road ice cream and a hilarious movie."

"No, thank you. I just want to be alone."

"It'll be better in the morning… you'll see."

Before she leaves, she closes my heavy curtains to block out the sun and its false warmth.

Discoveries

I lift my eyes to the heavens, and observe the black velvety feathers drifting to the ground from the grey storm clouds. Soon several accumulate in my outstretched hand and darken my hair.

I notice, in the distance, a headstone with no name engraved in its granite. Before I can approach it, I hear whispers coming from behind me. Suddenly, somebody grasps my neck and squeezes until I can no longer bring oxygen to my lungs and blackness swallows me.

My head shoots up as I suck in air. I look around my room and wipe my face with my hands.

"Ann? Are you awake?" Christian asks as he closes the door.

"Christian? What time is it? What are you doing in here?"

I rub my eyes trying to push my nightmare out of my brain fog.

"Could you turn the light on, please?"

The brightness makes my eyes water but helps the fog clear.

"Ann, please explain to me, what happened?"

"Christian, what do you mean?"

"What happened with you and Ryan earlier? Why are you leaving the Palace sooner than you intended?"

I look away from his intense gaze. "It just isn't working out between us."

"Why isn't it working out, Ann?"

"Because it just isn't, okay. Let's just drop it and go back to bed."

He moves his face closer to mine, searching my eyes. He places his hand on the back of my head and brings my lips to his. Shock racks my body and I know I should pull away from his hungry lips. But being back in his arms feels right in a world that is going to hell in a handbasket.

When he pulls away, I wrap my arms around his neck, tugging him closer to me and deepening the kiss. I want to tell him about all the secrets, and do what I know is right, but I don't want to hurt him in the process.

My brain screams over how wrong our embrace is, but my body craves his closeness and an escape from Ryan's and Mary's secrets, even if it's just for a moment.

I pull back and stare into his icy eyes. Those eyes. They remind me of warm, cloudless summer days filled with excitement and wonder.

We've never had secrets between us, other than his dad's craziness. Would he really care that his brother and fiancée did what they did to save me?

"Ann, tell me what's going on in your head? You look as if you are thousands of miles away from me." He rests his forehead on mine.

I shake the thoughts from my head. "I'm just surprised that's all. Why did you kiss me, Christian? You are engaged to Mary."

"I thought, perhaps, you were departing because you couldn't bear the thought of Mary and me getting married. And to be completely honest, I wanted to feel that passion again. I'm sorry… you're right. I shouldn't have kissed you. I will control myself from now on. I swear to you, no more nonsense from me. You have my word."

I watch his eyes swirl with emotion. I nibble my bottom lip. Did he and Mary not have a physical connection? Surely, they must have strong feelings towards each other.

"Christian, do you love Mary?"

"You know, Ann, my father was always telling me what to do, what to think, and who I needed to love."

I think back to the same answer I had given Ryan not too long ago, regarding whom I loved.

"A wise man once asked me: who's the one person you see spending the rest of your life with. Someone you could tell anything to and do anything with. When you see them, you smile ear to ear, and you look forward to seeing them again when they're away?"

"What was your answer, Ann?"

"It wasn't easy to answer. I'm incredibly lucky to love a lot of people."

"Yes, I've noticed. It seems every time you walk out the door, you acquire a new admirer."

"Christian, you never answered my question. Do you love Mary?"

"I want to... I really do... but there's something going on with her that I can't understand. She's concealing something from me, and it's pushing us further and further apart."

I feel the words forming at the tip of my tongue, but I clamp down on them.

My poker face fails me.

"Ann, tell me what you know."

I look around the room, unsure if this is a safe place. I glance towards the balcony. "Will you walk outside with me?"

We both stare into the chilly night air. I shiver in my silk night gown as I glance at the crescent moon. He wraps his arm around me and pulls me to his chest. His steady heartbeat calms my nerves. "What is it, Ann? You know you can tell me anything."

Can I tell him? This will change everything.

As I look deep into his eyes, I know what I must do, no matter the consequences. "Christian, would you kill to save my life?"

"Is somebody threatening you?"

"Just answer the question, please."

"Yes, I'd take a life to save your life, Ann."

"Even if you had to murder a member of your family?"

"Where are you going with this?"

All I hear in the cool night air are the birds settling for the night. The silence is deafening as I try to word this as gently as possible.

"I need you to promise me that whatever I say to you, you'll think it through and sit here before anything else."

"Yes, Ann. You have my word."

I pull out a chair for him, letting him know I'm serious. I look around again and decide to take extra precautions. I kneel next to him and put my lips to his ear. "Your dad was poisoned by an untraceable herb and I know who did it."

Christian jumps up, oblivious to the crashing of the chair to the ground beneath him. My heart leaps into my throat as I glance towards the doorway.

I catch his wrist, stopping him from bolting. He glares at me as he yanks his arm away, as if I had burned him.

"But the test was negative, and I told you everything. How long have you known?" His words stab at my heart.

"I only found out a few hours ago. I thought something was wrong with how Lady Mary was rushing the wedding, so I was poking around and found out this information."

He runs his hands through his dirty blonde hair and paces. "Who else knows about this?"

I hold my breath. I was hoping he wasn't going to ask this. When I don't answer, he stops pacing and arches a brow.

"Ann?"

"A couple of people."

"What people know, Ann?"

"Christian, does it really matter? They were pressured into it because of Mary. It was her idea, and she alone was the one who thought and acted on it."

His fingertips dig into my shoulders. "Who else?"

"A handful of servants—and your brother. Christian, please, tell me what you're thinking. Did I make a mistake by telling you?"

"Ann, how can you say that? We are a team. We're always honest with each other, no matter what." He rubs his face. "To be honest, I'm furious with *myself*." He sits in the chair. "I knew Mary was acting peculiar when she worked extremely hard at keeping me in the hospital wing with Vinny. Then after my dad died, she was acting like she was distraught, but I could see right through it."

"Don't do that, Christian. Please, don't blame yourself." I rest a hand on his leg.

Tears form in the corners of his eyes. "I can't believe my own brother didn't tell me what happened to dad." He sighs. "I presume he informed you and didn't want you to tell me. Was that why he lied to me and stated you were going home?"

"Yes."

"Thank you for informing me, Ann." He wipes his eyes and whispers to the moon, "What should I do now?" He takes in a steadying breath, and I can tell he is trying to rein in his anger, as he clenches his hands into fists.

"Well, if you are looking for advice, I was thinking you have two options: either confront them, or pretend you don't know and see how far it goes."

He closes his eyes and massages his temples. "Ignoring them and pretending could be dangerous, especially if Mary still has some of that poison left." He shakes his head. "Ann, she could try to kill you with it out of spite. Or any one of us. I need to test her loyalty and make sure she is who she says she is."

"Christian, do you think…" I rub my hands, trying to get the picture of Mary and Ryan together in his room out of my head. "Do you think that Mary and Ryan maybe… have been…" I let the words fall between us.

"Ann, your guess is as good as mine at this moment. We'll have to confront them and go from there. What they've done is wrong, but I can't say that I wouldn't have done the same to save you or my family. Dad had no problem manipulating people or killing to get his way. That's probably why Ryan and Mary have been behaving irregularly. I'm sure that keeping this secret from us has been eating them alive. I'm glad that I can breathe a sigh of relief and not continually look over my shoulder. Get some rest, Ann, and tomorrow we'll meet with them and get this over with."

I watch him walk out, his back hunched. Even though Christian and I have a complicated relationship, my heart aches to see him like this. I wish I could take away his pain.

I lean against the wall and wrap my arms around myself. I should feel relieved that this secret is out in the open. So why do I feel like my heart has been slashed into pieces?

I tilt my head as I hear scratching in the hallway. Slowly, I crack the door open while my eyes scan the darkness. Not seeing anybody, I move to close the door but leap back as something taps my foot.

I land with a hard thud on my butt.

"Snowball? What are you doing away from Elizabeth?"

Snowball tilts her head, as if to mock my clumsiness. Then she struts to my bed and flaps up onto the comforter and settles.

"Fine you can sleep with me tonight. But in the morning, you need to return to Elizabeth."

After I settle under the covers, I drape an arm around her and drift off to sleep.

Before Elizabeth wakes up the next morning, I slip Snowball inside her bedroom, unnoticed. Then I decide to eat my biscuits and gravy in my room with my dad, while watching the sunrise on the balcony.

After breakfast, dad goes to the support group meeting, while I go to the office. When I walk in, I'm surprised to see Ryan and Christian already there. They both turn to me and Ryan frowns. I look away from him and sit at the table. When Mary comes in, Christian asks her to take a seat, and he closes the door.

Christian clears his throat. "This room's secure to speak in, and I do encourage you all to be honest." He glares at Ryan and Mary, who glance at each other and then to me. "Don't you two blame Ann for your actions. At this point, she's the only person I trust." He crosses his arms over his chest. "Mary, explain to me, what happened the night that my father died."

"Christian, you know your father had been threatening my family if I didn't marry you." She swallows. "I was worried he would never stop. That one day, I would wake up to my family's sudden disappearance. So, I did some research and found this herb. With it, I could make a tainted, tasteless beverage. A few hours after someone drinks it, they experience heart failure. After I found the herb, I lost my nerve and put it away, knowing I could never go through with it and have the King's death on my hands." A tear rolls down her face. "Then when I found out the King had Derek imprison Ann, planned on murdering her, and blaming her death on the guard that was stabbed, I panicked. I didn't want any more innocent lives being hurt because of your father."

My face pales. "He was going to blame my death on Vinny?"

Mary replies, "I think he was trying to get your maid involved in the plot too, because she was too close to you."

"Did anybody assist you with this plan of action?" Christian asks.

Ryan turns to Christian. "I helped Mary get the herb into dad's night cap."

Christian blinks at Ryan. "How did you accomplish that, Ryan? You were on bed rest."

Ryan looks down at his hands. "I asked dad to come talk to me before he went to bed. He came in with his drink and set it on my nightstand. While he lectured about how unimportant Ann was and reminded me this was for the good of the family, and in turn the country, I slipped it into his drink." He looks at Christian before continuing, "It wasn't an easy decision, Christian, but I wasn't going to let him take Ann away from me. And I'd do it again in a heartbeat. I'll take your punishment without regret."

Christian looks to Mary. "And you? Do you regret it?"

She squirms. "Christian, I regret hurting you, but all in all, I don't regret my decision."

"Thank you for your honesty. I need you both to vow that you will never, *ever*, keep anything from me again. We're a team here, and in order to keep this country running, we need each other." Everyone sighs and leans back in their chairs. "Before I pass my final judgment, you'll be required to take a lie detector test to prove your innocence and loyalty, understood? It's going to take some time to gain my trust back. And the wedding *will* be postponed until further notice."

"Christian, what about mom? Should we tell her?" Ryan asks.

Christian closes his eyes. "No, we'll just keep it between us and take it to our graves." He opens his eyes and leans back.

"Mom is already suspicious of Mary— are you sure that's a good idea?" Ryan leans forward.

"I'm certain that with the postponing of the wedding and redirecting Mary and mom to work together on the arrangements for the ball, we can smooth those suspicions over."

Vinny steps in with his arms crossed over his chest and a 'do not mess with me' attitude.

"Vinny will take you to your lie detector tests."

We stand and walk towards Vinny.

"Ann, please stay behind with me."

Christian hands Vinny a list of questions and tells him to call if there are any problems. Vinny nods and closes the door behind them. I let out a breath as I crash back into the chair.

"What the hell was all that?"

"More secrets revealed." He stares into space. "Ann, do you think we can trust them?"

I look into his icy eyes. "Your fiancée's a murderer, and my best friend was an accomplice." I laugh at the absurdity. "And both of them say it was to save *my* life." I shake my head. "How do you react to that?"

He grabs my hand. "You thank your lucky stars and be grateful that you have another day, while appreciating those around you who care about you." He smirks. "Care enough to literally kill for you."

I blink. Was I hearing things? Did Christian the stoic just freaken make a joke *right* now?

"Christian…"

"How about we take a stroll to clear our minds, Ann?"

We walk into the early afternoon sun, and even with its rays reaching out, the breeze chills me while I twirl a golden leaf between my fingers.

"Are you really going to let Mary go that easily, Christian?"

"What do you propose I do, Ann? Throw her against the wall and choke her like I did to you, when I was seeing beyond red? I'm trying to be mature and merciful, and you are questioning me? The very same woman who convinced the King and Queen to free-range the Palace chickens, just so a flock of birds can live a happier life?"

"But Mary orchestrated this whole thing."

"Yes, she did, and the lie detector test will provide us with the evidence we need to convict her."

"Are you still going to marry her?"

Christian plucks the leaf out of my hand, pulling my attention to his eyes.

"Do you realize what would happen if I don't marry her, Ann?"

"You get to fluff your feathers for a new group of lucky ladies?"

"Fluff my feathers?" He shakes his head. "It doesn't work that way, Ann. We only get one group of single women to choose from. Which means if Mary doesn't marry me, I would wed the next contestant, the runner-up before her."

His words wash over me. That is me.

"So, you see, I'm—how do you say—between a rock and a hard place."

I clear my throat and start walking towards the chicken coop.

"What do you think?"

"It looks wonderful. I think the ribbon-cutting ceremony will be occurring soon."

"Are you teasing me?"

He chuckles. "It looks incredible, Ann. I look forward to the improvement of our egg and poultry numbers. And hopefully offsetting the expenses." He gives me a stern business look.

"O, ye of little faith." I bump him with my shoulder.

"I still don't understand why we had to pay out so much, when the other one was working perfectly."

I roll my eyes as I remember how different we are. The old pen was not free-range, and the chickens were living in small cages. Whereas now they are free, happy, and organic. Oh, how we see the world differently.

I let the argument drop off my lips.

We stroll through the flower garden and Christian plucks off a vibrant blue flower and slides it behind my ear.

"What is this flower called?"

"These plants are resilient and often overlooked. They are called Forget-Me-Nots. I know they don't look as lovely as your cherished roses, but they are one of my favorites in the garden."

Christian looks up into the cloudless sky. "Ann, do you think my dad had any good in him?"

I watch the conflict burn behind his eyes, so I select my words carefully.

"I think your dad had good intentions, but he didn't have the best ways of obtaining them."

Moving Forward

Christian scans over Vinny's reports and nods.

"It seems your stories check out, and now we can begin to rebuild our trust." He looks up at Mary. "We need to talk, privately." Then he swivels to us. "Ryan, now would be a wonderful time to show Ann the lake house and discuss what's been going on."

I frown. "But, Christian, we can't go on a vacation right now. My dad is here, and we have work to catch up on."

"Ann, this is far more important than office work, and it is *not* a request." He stands and we all join him. "Let's agree to never speak of this incident again. We have examined it and are moving on with our lives. Does everyone understand me?" We look around at each other, our little alliance, and nod. "Good, you're dismissed."

Ryan grabs my elbow. "Listen, Ann—"

I put a hand up. "Not now, okay? I'm getting a migraine."

He frowns but releases the grip on my arm. "Are you going to meet me downstairs?"

"Do you *really* think it's a good idea to go anywhere with me right now?" I cross my arms over my chest.

His lips quirk. "I can take the wrath of Ann."

"Well, I don't want to go anywhere with you."

"But Christian asked us to."

"So what?"

"Are you a rule breaker now? Well, I can be just as immature as you. I'm going to go tattle on you." He pivots and walks away.

"Fine! I'll meet you downstairs."

I stomp into my room and run into Karen. She smiles up at me as she packs a bag. "What's this, Karen?"

"Christian called and asked me to pack you an overnight bag."

"Why would he do that?"

"Christian said you and Ryan were going to go to the lake house and stay the night together." She wiggles her eyebrows.

I grumble as I change into something warm and comfortable.

Karen arches her brow. "So, I take it you are not a willing participant?"

I catch her up on what has happened.

"Sweetie, life is messy. But at least Ryan is willing to talk through the mess with you. You know, he could just give you the cold shoulder and walk away."

I grab my bag and make my way down the stairs. I know Karen is right, but it doesn't make Ryan's actions hurt any less.

I see Ryan standing by his car and I can't help but pause at his jeans and tight green tee shirt. He could almost pass as a normal guy.

"Lady Ann." He bows.

"Prince Ryan."

As we get on the road, he turns to me. "Can we talk?"

"What would you like to talk about?"

He snorts. "Come on, I'm attempting to fix things between us."

The view changes from tall city skyscrapers to a green wilderness before my eyes. I roll the window down and breathe in the fresh air. Memories of home flood my mind. I wonder what the chickens are doing right now. Was Suzie making sure they had enough grit and oyster shell for their eggs?

When we arrive at the little log cabin, I admire the architecture of the A-frame style and lush surroundings.

Behind the house is a glittering lake. The water's path is so long that I can't see where it begins or ends as I observe ducks calling to each other in the distance.

I hear the grass crunch as Ryan steps beside me.

"It is beautiful, isn't it?" He elbows me. "Remember when you rescued that duckling?"

Ryan's words pull me back to the day Pecker died. We stopped to get some burgers and then sat at a rest area to eat. Nearby a duckling had trash wrapped around its neck and Ryan saved its life.

My eyes focus back on the present and I rub my chilled arms.

"The inside of the cabin doesn't compare to this natural beauty, but it's warmer and has a fireplace."

The house is small but has a roaring fire in the living room with couches in front of it. The kitchen is stocked and has a state-of-the-art coffee machine on the counter.

"Do you want to see our room?"

"Room? As in one?" I squeak out.

He laughs. "The one downside to this place, is yes, it only has one bedroom."

We walk into the large bedroom with an attached closet and bathroom.

"So, I guess you are sleeping on the couch?" I arch a brow at Ryan.

"I am too tall for the couch." He falls back on the king-size bed and sprawls out. "I'm willing to share the bed with you, Ann."

I roll my eyes. "No, thank you. I will sleep on the couch."

I turn to leave but he comes up behind me and spins me around. I stare into his dark eyes and swallow.

"Don't push me away, Ann. Please." He rubs his fingertips down my jawline as he searches my eyes. "I need my friend back. Tell me what I have to do so we can move past this?"

I jerk back. "This? This! You helped murder someone! Not just anyone but your father!"

"But it was for you!" he shouts. "Everything I did was for you!" He steps back. "I'm glad everything is out in the open. Because keeping this secret from you and Christian has been the hardest thing I've ever done." He brushes past me and starts to unpack his bag.

I slide the porch door open and look around the backyard. My feet creak as I walk on the deck overlooking the lake. I lower myself on a soft wooden chair and watch the birds play in the water.

I suck in a breath and shiver as a breeze tosses my hair around. Oh, how I am going to miss the warmer weather once winter hits.

Ryan sets down a box of pizza and a chocolate bar on the table in front of me.

"Thought you might be getting hungry."

"Where did you get this?"

"Well, it's this magical thing called *delivery*," he teases as he opens the box.

My mouth waters as the smell wafts towards me. I snatch a slice and begin to chew the hot cheesy goodness. After the pizza is almost gone, I grab the chocolate bar and turn to him. "Thank you."

We watch the sun paint bright orange and blue hues across the night sky. Once its warmth is gone, we both huddle inside by the fireplace.

Ryan pulls me to him and kisses my cheek. I rest my head on his shoulder as I watch the fire consume the logs. Then he runs his hand lazily up and down my arm.

Before my lids get heavy, I sigh and think to myself—this is how married life should feel, comfortable, peaceful, and safe.

I wake up in the middle of the night with Ryan snoring next to me on the couch. I stretch and groan.

"Is everything okay?"

"My neck is sore." I turn it from side to side.

He positions his hands on my neck and gently massages it. I moan as the muscles warm and the tension subsides. He leans in and places soft kisses where he had been rubbing.

I shiver as tiny tingles run down my back. Soon his mouth moves from my neck to my cheek. Then he lingers over my lips. I close the gap and once our mouths touch, I feel a warm sensation pass over my body. He embraces me and deepens the kiss.

The passion is overwhelming, and I have to gently pull away and take a labored breath.

He watches me with dark eyes. "I would say I'm sorry, but that would be a lie."

"Where did that come from, Ryan? You told me you don't want to be a couple, then this!"

"I was afraid to lose you as a friend. You saw what happened to Cherie and me."

"Ryan, look at everything that has happened to us, and I am still here."

He sits next to me. "I guess we just need time to regain our bearings, huh?"

I walk to the bedroom while he watches me.

"Are you coming?"

"Ann, I thought I was sleeping on the couch?"

"Well, suit yourself, but that bed is big enough to share… and yet, distance ourselves."

I wiggle under the covers, wishing that this place had central heat and not just a fireplace. It's not like they can't afford it.

I turn to see Ryan walk in to the bathroom to get ready for bed. Then he silently slips in on the opposite side of me.

I inch closer to his warmth but stop short as my eyes shoot open.

"Ryan, where's your shirt?"

"I don't like wearing shirts to bed."

I feel the heat radiating from his back and the temptation is too much. "But it's freezing outside."

He turns to me and smirks. "You know, if you don't want to wear a shirt to bed too, I will completely understand."

I swat his arm. "I'm going to tell my dad you suggested that."

He pulls me to him. "Although your baldness is a major turn off."

I kick him. "It's not that bad. Hey, Ryan, are we starting a relationship? Like boyfriend and girlfriend?"

He tenses and pulls back, realizing the mixed signals he has been sending me. "I'm sorry, Ann, I just... I need more time." He turns away from me.

My eyes prick as I blink at his back. I want to pry and argue, but I turn away from him as a silent tear falls.

Am I not good enough for him? What am I doing wrong?

I wipe the tear away and resolve to focus on work and getting ready to head back home to my chickens. No more boyfriend drama. We are only friends.

That's it.

In the morning, we eat a quick breakfast together, pack, and head back to the Palace.

"Ann, about last night…" Ryan says as we start our drive.

"Don't worry, Ryan. I get it. We are only friends. You don't want to date me because of my bald spot."

The silence extends as I watch the trees turn into structures once again.

"It's not you. It's me. Cherie hurt me. And I'm still not confident that Christian has moved on. Plus, I feel like I'm again taking second place to my older brother." He groans and leans back. "You know? Like getting his leftovers," he grumbles.

I turn to him mouth agape. "Are you kidding me? Did you just call me *leftovers*?"

He groans as he focuses on pulling into the Palace gate. "Ann, I didn't mean it like that. Although, you tasted rather good last night." He winks as he parks his car.

I stomp inside the Palace, passing servants as I go. I bypass Tim and go directly into Christian's office. He glances up from a folder.

"Ann, it's nice to have you back. How was your night?"

"Why did you do it?" I spit every syllable at his smug face.

"Do what exactly?" He quirks a brow.

"Shove your brother and me into a small cabin with no heat and only one bed."

He shrugs. "I thought it was obvious. I wanted you two to work things out."

"He doesn't want me you big matchmaking idiot! Are you happy now?" I glare as a tear slips out. "He called me your leftovers." I turn to leave but he catches my arm.

"Ann, please, my intentions were honorable. I didn't know he wasn't interested in you."

I pull my arm away and narrow my eyes. "Well, he isn't, so stop pushing us together."

"I'm sorry, Ann. I never meant to hurt you."

"That seems like all you ever do to me—hurt me."

"That was never my intention," he whispers softly.

I swipe at my eyes and change the topic. "Any word on the wedding? The sooner you guys get back from your honeymoon, the sooner I can leave."

"Mom is on board with us having the wedding sooner rather than later. She and Mary have been planning and shopping all day."

I grab the doorknob and look up at him. "Congratulations, Christian. I'm happy for you two. You deserve to be happy."

I run to Karen for a hug and I update her on my night.

"Ann, I'm sorry. I know Ryan cares about you. He is just too afraid."

"How are you and Vinny?"

She catches me up on their lives, and how thrilled they are about their home being constructed. It was nice to listen to a normal couple's problems and enthusiasm.

There is a knock on the door and Tim pops his head in.

"Lady Ann, the King has some forms he would like you to read through and sign."

"Of course." I turn to Karen. "I will see you soon."

I grumble at the stack of folders on my desk—back to work. As I read through them, make notes, and sign them, Ryan walks over. I glance up mid-sentence, with a pencil in my mouth as I edit.

"How does that taste?" He smirks.

I remove the mangled wood from my mouth. "Better than you do."

"Ouch." He offers me a box. "Here's a peace offering." Then he sits down in the chair across from me and opens his own.

I push the small parcel back to him. "No, thank you. I don't want to be an inconvenience to you, Prince Ryan."

He quirks a brow as he bites into his sandwich. "By eating the food that I brought you?"

I grab my pencil and start reading again, feeling his eyes on me.

"Ann, come on. Don't you think you're being a little sensitive?"

"You have mustard on your chin."

He dabs it with a napkin. "I guess I was saving it for later."

"Oh, so you're okay with *those* leftovers?"

He crosses his arms over his chest, and I try not to notice how tight that gesture makes his shirt.

"I was trying to be honest with you, Ann."

"The truth hurts apparently."

Once I hear the clicks of his keyboard, I peek inside the package. It's one of my favorites, roast beef and cheese with spicy tortilla chips. Once I finish it, I pick up my phone and dial his desk.

"Prince Ryan," he says as he twirls in his chair.

"You are still a jerk, but thank you for lunch."

The paperwork takes most of the day and by the time I stand and stretch, not many people are left in the office. I make my rounds and turn in the signed forms to the respective departments. When I get to finance, I'm surprised to see Kevin still sitting there. I slap down a folder and his eyes dart up from his computer screen.

"Lady Ann, nice to see you working finally."

"Just dropping off the order forms for the ball."

He groans. "Is it already that time?" Then he files the folder for finalization tomorrow.

"You don't like to dance?"

"I don't like the hype and pressure that surrounds it."

"I love the music, food, and decorations..." My eyes glaze over.

He watches me, smiling. "I'm glad someone likes it."

"Have a good night, Kevin."

When I'm ready to walk out, I bump into Kevin on the way. "Sorry, ladies first." He bows and lets me pass.

I run into Ryan outside the office doors.

"What was that about?" he asks.

"What was what about, Ryan?"

"I saw you talking to Kevin earlier and then again just now."

"Ryan, we work together, remember?"

"But he likes you."

"At least someone does."

"I like you."

"Not enough apparently."

I trudge to my room and shut the door loud enough for him to hear my aggravation. When did Ryan morph into a Christian Jr.? It was getting ridiculous. I don't have to explain myself every time I talk to somebody of the opposite sex.

I glide my brush through my hair prior to heading to dinner. I'm eager to see my dad after a long day at the office. I hope Christian is true to his word and is giving him a king's vacation.

I hug my dad before I sit down and stab my lamb chop.

"How was your day, dad?"

"I went to this little lake house and fished most of the day. And I caught some of the biggest fish I have ever seen. Then I sat in front of a roaring fireplace with my feet up and napped. I have never felt so relaxed."

"I'm thrilled you are enjoying your vacation. Are you planning on prolonging your visit and staying for the wedding, dad?"

"Yes, then I intend to start my retirement, and travel north afterwards. When are you heading back home, Ann?" he asks between bites.

"As soon as I can."

"What about traveling with me?" Ryan pouts.

"Ryan, I don't think that's a great idea, considering the recent events."

After dinner, my dad and I go for a stroll and he updates me on his adventures with Elizabeth, while I show him the inside of the Palace and all of its amenities.

Afterwards, I return to my room to shower, and I am surprised to see Ryan sitting on my bed.

"I was hoping we could talk, Ann."

I roll my eyes as I walk towards the bathroom and remove my make-up. "You don't want your brother's leftovers—I get it. No need to explain yourself."

"Can't we resume our friendship?"

I watch him draw closer to me in the mirror. He grabs my hairbrush and runs it through my hair.

"Ryan, I want more than a friendship with you."

"So, you won't even try to be friends?"

My fingers instinctively go to my lips as I remember the many kisses we have shared. I turn and look deep into his eyes while I wrap my arms around his neck.

"Tell me you don't want me to touch you, that you don't want to have me by your side every day, and I'll stop."

He swallows as he looks down at my lips. "I… you aren't being fair."

I close the gap between us and our lips touch. When he doesn't return the kiss, I pull away, but he groans and wraps his arms around my waist and tugs me into him. He deepens the kiss and holds me close.

"Why are you fighting this, Ryan?" I say breathlessly.

"Because I can't deal with another heartache, Ann." He pulls away and pushes his hands through his hair. "Why do you keep ignoring my wishes and pressing the issue?"

"Because I know you are making a terrible mistake. How do you know it'll be the same?"

"I'm not willing to take that risk. I'm sorry, Ann. And if you can't let it go, then we can't be friends."

The door closes and I am left alone, in pain. I pushed myself on him and was turned down, again. The one person I thought would always be there for me...

Wedding Bells

As the wedding draws near, Mary humors me and requests that I be one of her bridesmaids. And her brother Max and Ryan are groomsmen. I am relieved that she has paired me with her brother Max and not Ryan, because I don't think that would have helped our situation. After the wedding, we have the coronation for Mary then the reception.

"Ann, you look beautiful," my dad praises. "You look so much like your mother with your hair like that."

"Thank you, dad. You clean up nice too."

"Take it easy, young lady," he gestures towards my champagne flute.

"Yes, sir," I salute.

The color white surrounds me—streamers, balloons, and flowers. I sigh as I watch Christian and Mary glide across the dance floor. I gulp down my drink, making my eyes water. I'm glad he chose her. They really do look great together.

I set my empty glass down as Max strides over and presents me with another one. I smile at the younger man and accept his generous gift. I sip it while his eyes wash over me shamelessly.

He is tall with brown hair and sparkling green eyes—mesmerizing. I blink and turn away from his gaze.

"For such a gorgeous woman, I am surprised you're not out there dancing with somebody."

"Max, I appreciate the compliment but I'm too old for you."

He steps closer to me and I can tell he is tipsy. "Not by much. What, two years?"

"You're incredibly sweet, Max, but try four or five years."

"Age is just a number, sweetheart." He caresses my hand. "Come on. Give me just one dance."

"Lady Ann, it was a great ceremony, wasn't it?" Mary smiles at us.

"Yes, the best one I've ever had the privilege of participating in."

I hold back the fact that it is the *only* wedding I have ever been in. As I sip my wine, I hide a smirk behind the rim while Mary glares at Max. Obviously, she does not approve of Max and me dancing—thank God. I want nothing to do with her or her family.

Mary offers a hand to Max. "How about you dance with your Queen?"

He mumbles incoherently but offers his arm with a promise to return. When they are at a safe distance, I turn to leave and crash into Christian's hard chest.

"Sorry, Christian… my King."

He laughs. "It's fine, Lady Ann. Was that Mary, dragging Max to the dance floor?"

"Yes, it was—Max was trying to convince me to dance with him, and when I turned him down, he wouldn't let it go."

"Do you want me to speak with him?"

"I'm a big girl. I can handle it."

"Would you deny your King a dance?"

"I don't think that's a great idea."

"Your drink isn't a good idea." He quirks a brow.

"Why? Is Kevin around?" I tease—remembering the last time that I drank, I almost went home with Kevin.

"He's probably lurking in the shadows, getting ready to pounce."

"And where's your brother?"

"He is dancing with Mary's cousin Courtney."

I look towards the dance floor and I frown, observing Ryan slow dancing with a blonde woman. "Well, he looks like he's having fun." I down my drink.

"Ann, are you okay?" Christian watches me.

"Oh, yeah, I'm just peachy," I retort.

I find an isolated bench to sit on to clear my thoughts. I place my head in my hands, trying to erase the image of Ryan with another woman.

"You look like you could use a friend."

"Dan? What are you doing here?"

"I was somehow invited. I've never seen an event this elegant before. My entire salary probably wouldn't even cover the food. I guess it was a pity invite. But how do you turn this down?"

"So, why aren't you enjoying yourself, and dancing?"

"I haven't found the right partner yet."

He reaches for my hand.

"Dan, I don't think that is a good idea."

"It's just a dance, Ann. Look, even your dad is out there."

I snap my head back. There, in the center of the dance floor, is my dad slow dancing with Elizabeth.

Dan sits next to me and places a hand on mine. "Ann, I can't imagine how hard this is for you. To witness Christian getting married and being a part of the wedding. Then watching Ryan dance with another woman. I'd say it's time for you to have a turn, huh?" He offers his hand again. "I promise no kissing or inappropriate touching."

"Dan, why are you always so kind to me?"

"A wise woman once told me that this world needs a little more compassion."

He paraphrases what I said when we met last year.

"No kissing or inappropriate touching?"

"Scout's honor."

I allow him to guide me towards the dance floor. I giggle as they play the chicken dance and the macarena.

After a few songs, I'm laughing and watching Dan make an idiot out of himself.

"Aren't you glad you joined in on the fun?" he yells over the music.

"I am glad I didn't miss seeing you do the chicken dance."

"I think I was pretty impressive."

"But you couldn't remember the moves."

"But I was darn good at going with the flow."

As the music changes to a love song, I walk off, but Dan pulls me into him with a smile. I blush as I allow him to move closer to me and wrap his arm around my waist. "Too close?" he asks against my ear.

I lean my tired head on his shoulder, and he holds me tighter. We sway to the music, enjoying each other's company.

It is nice, just going with the flow and letting him take the lead. Plus, I don't mind the secure hold he has on my waist. Dan is confident and he knows what he wants. There is no confusion or hesitation in his actions, and he is very respectful.

When the song ends, Dan pulls back and turns to see Ryan cutting in. Dan forces a smile and allows Ryan to take his place.

"What the hell is wrong with you, Ryan?"

"I am saving you from the construction worker. Who even invited him anyway?"

I push him away and march off the dance floor.

"Ann, what did I do now?" He grabs my arm.

"I was having fun dancing with the *contractor* Dan, and you ruined it."

"Really? You and Dan?"

"What about you and Mary's cousin?"

"You're keeping tabs on me?"

"Apparently, that is what you are doing to me," I retort, arms crossed over my chest.

A shadow passes over his eyes. "Please uncross your arms. You are showing a lot."

I blush as I notice this dress shows too much when prompted. I drop my arms. "Are you done giving me a hard time? Can I go back to Dan now?"

"You would rather be with him, than me?"

"Yes, because he actually wants to be with me, Ryan."

"I want to be friends."

"Fine, whatever, let's be friends. Now excuse me, I want to dance with Dan. Someone who wants more than a friendship."

"But I—"

"You what?"

He rubs his hands over his face. "Why can't we dance as friends?"

I can tell he isn't going to drop this, and I am not in the mood to keep going around in circles.

He leads me back onto the dance floor and pulls me close. We dance and I soon relax in his embrace.

"Ryan, you can't keep doing this to me."

"Doing what?"

"Telling me you don't want a relationship, then stopping me from having one with someone who does. It's not fair."

"You know, Dan could have said no when I cut in."

"Yes, deny his Prince and employer, that would look good." I roll my eyes.

"I see what you mean. I'll bring you back to him, if that's what you want?"

"Ryan, you know what I want." I look into his dark eyes.

"I'll escort you to him before I go back inside the Palace."

"No, I am done with all this excitement."

When I walk off the dance floor, I spot Snowball on her lead in a silk baby blue dress. I squint and see that her feathers are fluffed and that her nails are painted.

I remember the day I met Elizabeth. She had admitted she had always wanted a daughter, and now it looks like she has one. Although this one wears feathers, the love and companionship Snowball extends is the same.

I stroll into my room and observe Karen as she puts clothes away. I update her on the events of the night.

"Did you have a fun time though?"

"I did but now I'm exhausted, and tomorrow starts the craziness of Ryan and me running the country while Christian and Mary are off on their honeymoon."

Karen grins as she waves around chocolate candy and a chick flick.

"Good thing I came prepared! And there is a hot bath waiting for you."

That night, I dream of dancing with chickens in top hats while chocolate chips rain down from the sky, and it makes my mood lighter. When the early morning light seeps through, I feel ready to conquer the world.

"Good Morning," I sing.

Dad and Elizabeth look up and smile. "Good morning, Ann."

The butler fills my coffee cup and I take a long sip. As I look over the rim, I see Ryan coming in with dark circles under his eyes.

"Morning, sleeping beauty," I say.

He slurps his coffee. "Don't start. I slept like crap. I had nightmares all night."

I take a bite of my eggs. "I wonder why."

"It's because you continue to guilt trip me for not wanting to date you. And it is driving my dreams to torture me."

I feel my cheeks get hot as I hear my dad clear his throat and pretend to ignore our conversation.

"Sounds like you feel guilty, Ryan."

He glares at me.

After breakfast, we say goodbye to my dad before he starts his adventure.

"I'm going to miss you. Are you going to be home for Christmas?"

"I wish I could, Ann, but I promise next Christmas at our house will be the best ever."

I frown as he turns to hug Ryan, and then Elizabeth. I watch as they hug a little too long, and I observe the way he looks into her eyes and in response, how she blushes.

"Goodbye, Jack, drive safe," Elizabeth says.

"I'll call often and don't forget to join me later."

"Let me escort you to the car."

Then they go out together.

In the office, Ryan and I are bombarded with paperwork, phone calls, and appointments until well past lunchtime.

When I look up again, I see Max and I yelp.

"Max? What are you doing here?"

"I'm getting ready to head back home, but I wanted to stop in and give you these."

Then he hands me a bouquet of red roses in a pink glass vase.

"Thank you, Max, they are beautiful. But I can't accept these from you."

"Listen, Lady Ann, I'm sorry for my behavior last night. I may have had too much to drink."

"It's okay. I have been there, trust me."

He watches me move a loose strand of hair behind my ear.

"I was going to grab a bite to eat in the dining hall before I left. Would you like to join me?"

"Do you like sandwiches?"

"Who doesn't like sandwiches?"

I walk his way as he offers his arm. I accept it and swivel to Ryan, who is glaring at his computer screen.

"Ryan, we're going to get some lunch. Do you want something?"

He looks up and drops his pen at the sight of Max. "No, thanks."

I walk Max down the stairs and towards the servants' breakroom, a hidden gem in the Palace. He quirks a brow but lets me lead him inside.

"What is this place?" he asks as he looks around.

"It is the servants' breakroom."

"This is definitely more my level." And he laughs. "No offense."

We pull out sandwich supplies, sodas, and chips and begin assembling our plates. "None taken. I know that the Palace life can be overwhelming. I come from a farm four hours from here, so I know what you mean."

"You come from a farm? Really? But you look like you fit right in."

"Trust me, it took a long time for me to fit in. Didn't Mary tell you anything about me?"

"We don't talk much. I've actually learned more about you from the news reports."

"Please don't believe all that you hear. The news loves to embellish everything. Especially when it comes to me."

"I'm starting to realize that." He smiles as he writes his number down and passes it to me. "Maybe you can call me sometime? We can get to know each other more. You'll be returning home soon, right?"

"Yes, I'll be returning once the newlyweds come back."

"Good. No more crazy Palace life. More sandwiches and freedom. Thank you for allowing me to apologize, and for feeding me before I leave."

"Thank you for the apology flowers."

"Make sure you call me sometime, okay?"

"No promises, Max."

After I walk Max out to his car, I sit down in the office and Ryan stares up at me.

"Have fun with Mary's little brother?"

"Jealous?"

"A little… because now I want a sandwich," he pouts.

"Order one then, you big baby."

"But you make them better."

"How about you finish all of this paperwork and I'll make you a sandwich?"

"Nice try, but no. I would rather starve."

I go back to my pile, eyeing the flowers every so often, their smell reminding me of my young admirer.

After the to do list is complete, we slump out of the office and towards our rooms.

"Do you want to do something together tonight, Ann?"

I sigh, done playing his mind games. "No, thank you."

He stops short. "Why not?"

I pause with my hand on my doorknob.

"Ryan, I can be nice and a coworker, but I can't handle the closeness of a friendship right now with you." I sigh as he frowns. "I'm sorry. Just give me some more time."

Before I can close the door, Karen squeals.

"I heard you had flowers delivered today!"

"Yes, from Mary's younger brother Max."

"So what? Give me details!" She sits down on my bed, staring up at me.

"Why the sudden interest?"

"I'm always interested in your life, but now that I am married and fat, I need some extra gossip in my own life."

"You aren't fat. You are pregnant. There is a huge difference. Fine." I tell her about my lunch date and the flowers. "Then he gave me his phone number and told me to call him sometime."

"So, are you going to call him?"

"Karen, he's too young."

"Even more of a reason to say yes!" She winks at me.

"No, absolutely not."

"Then what about Dan? I heard you guys danced at the wedding."

"Are you keeping tabs on me?"

"Girl, everyone in the Palace is! They all want to know who you'll end up with."

My mouth drops. "Everyone?" I groan. "I can't wait to leave this circus and go home."

Ryan arrives with cheeseburgers and fries.

"And here is the clown now," I grumble.

He tilts his head as Karen shuts the door. "Clown?"

"What is this, Ryan?"

"It's food, Ann."

"I told you…"

"I know what you said, Ann, but it doesn't mean I have to agree with you. I want your friendship."

"You're being extremely stubborn."

"So are you, monkey."

"Monkey?"

"You said I was a clown. So, you are a monkey."

"I can't wait until Christian and Mary get back. All this extra work is killing my hands."

164

"It'll be weird when you leave us."

"You'll be traveling around the world. You won't even notice me gone."

"I'll notice because I made this trip for you to accompany me. Are you sure you won't go with me?"

"Yes, I am. It wouldn't be right. Plus, I am looking forward to going back home to my chickens and a normal life."

"When will I see you again?"

"Ryan, you'll see me tomorrow morning."

"You know what I mean. We'll have two separate lives, far apart. At least now, we get to see each other every day."

"You'll move on and find someone you trust and can live with."

"And you?"

"I'll remain a crazy chicken lady. Thank you for bringing me dinner."

"Anytime."

Karen glances over at me as the door shuts.

"Ryan looks miserable."

"I know, but I can't pretend I don't have feelings for him, Karen. If I stay, it'll only make it harder for me to leave when the time comes."

In the morning, I eat my breakfast in my room so I can have more time to clear my brain fog from last night.

Later, I sit at my desk and shuffle through my files and I line up today's agenda. As I move things around, my eyes fall on the flowers Max gave me and memories pull me away from the office, and to the spring days when my mom would run with me in our flower garden. We would laugh and roll in the grass, surrounded by fragrant beauties. We'd have picnics and read under the towering sunflowers' shade as bees buzzed around us. Then when we would come back inside the house, my dad would kiss our foreheads and tell us we were his favorite blooms of the season.

My phone rings and startles me out of my daydream. When I answer it, my busy workday begins.

At lunchtime, Elizabeth comes to my desk.

"Ann, my dear, we missed you at breakfast this morning."

"I woke up late. I'm sorry."

"It's okay. I was wondering when you were going to get fitted for your ball dress?"

"Oh, I'm actually heading home before Christmas. I'm leaving as soon as Christian comes back."

"I thought you would want to celebrate Christmas here, with us. Especially with your father away."

"I'm sorry, Elizabeth, but I promised Mary that when they returned, I would leave."

"But you'll be all alone."

"It's usually just dad and me for the holidays anyways. I'll survive. But I appreciate the offer."

She turns to Ryan, who looks away.

"You'll always be welcome back here." She hugs me as she tears up.

It is hard to get Elizabeth's sad face out of my head. She has become a surrogate mother to me this last year. And I will be forever grateful.

As I file the last folder, I turn to leave and jump back when I see Ryan staring at me.

"Ryan. Don't do that. You look like a stalker from a horror film."

"Ann, do you want to have dinner with us?"

I rub my temples. "I know this conversation is going to go round and round, until I say yes. So, I'm going to cut back the arguing and accept your offer."

I sit next to his mom as the roast is served. We talk about how exciting it'll be to have Christian back home. Then Elizabeth grins and tries to guess how long it'll be until Mary gets pregnant, while pondering over the gender of her first grandchild.

Soon we say goodnight and Ryan walks me to my room. At the door, he stops and just when I think he is going to say something more, he swallows and instead says, "Goodnight."

After that, time passes quickly and the day that Christian and Mary are set to arrive is filled with excitement all around. The maids clean with a pep in their step, the cooks go above and beyond with their meal preparations, and the office is buzzing with activity.

I finalize everything and leave my folders in their locations for the last time. I look towards my dying flowers and I toss them into the trash. I turn my head as I hear cheers in the hallway, and I see Christian and Mary walking together, hand in hand.

I sneak out unseen and as I walk into my room, I look around. Karen had packed while I was working, and my emotions stir at seeing all my belongings in boxes.

It is all too real. This is the end of my Palace life.

"Ann, are you okay?" Karen rubs my arm.

"Of course." I wipe my eyes. "When will you and Vinny be joining me?"

"Actually, our house will be ready ahead of schedule, so we'll be moving in there soon."

"That's wonderful news, Karen. You guys must be thrilled to start your new life. I can visit, right? And help you two set up the nursery?"

"You better help me. Because I don't know what the hell I'm doing."

Christian pops his head in. "Lady Ann, we didn't see you in the office."

"I finished early, and I wanted to get a start on packing."

"Are you planning on gracing us with your presence before you go? How about one final meal together?" He offers his arm, as if I have a choice.

"How was your honeymoon? Was it everything you had hoped for, and more?" I grin at his blush.

"Yes, it was. Thank you for asking."

When we walk in, I'm surprised to see a banner that reads, "We'll miss you, Lady Ann." I look around and see all the office staff, Vinny, and Karen sneaking in.

"Thank you, guys." I smile with tears brimming.

"You have done so much for me, for us all… We just wanted to give you a proper farewell celebration," Christian says as he leads me to my seat.

We eat cake and laugh as everyone says one thing that they will remember most about me. When it's

Christian's turn, he talks about my defiant attitude and my sprained ankle.

When it's Ryan's turn, everyone leans in as he stands. "I was sitting in the library one morning working on a report, bored out of my mind, when suddenly a beautiful woman walks in. And she, of course, completely ignores me, and goes straight to the bookshelves."

The evening wears down and everyone starts filing out. I shake hands and hug everyone as they leave and wish me well. I fall back into my chair, exhausted.

Christian hands me a box. "This is a small gift from our family."

I look around at all the people I'm going to miss.

"Thank you, you shouldn't have. Your friendship is a gift in itself." I open the box and gasp. "What's this?"

"We bought you a new car. That way, you can visit whenever you want," Elizabeth says.

"But I have a truck," I pout.

"Yes, but you need a reliable vehicle," Christian inserts.

The truck is old, and I doubt it will make it here and back. "Thank you. That's a very generous gift." My lip quivers as I look around and realize this might be the last time I'll ever be in the Palace. Each one of them has had an impact on my life, and it's hard to think of a life without them.

I open my arms wide, and everyone comes in for a group hug.

"Well, I'm going to hit the road before it gets too late."

I open my bedroom door one last time, surprised at how empty it now appears. Like it is ready for the next occupant, forgetting I was ever there.

Karen tilts her head. "Are you going to miss your room, Ann?"

"I'm going to miss the people that filled it. Did you get my Christmas presents set aside for everyone?"

She grins. "I have the pair of jeans for Christian, chicken accessories for Elizabeth, monogramed sketchbooks for Ryan, and a cute 'I am Queen B' wine glass for Mary."

I chuckle, imagining their faces on Christmas morning. "That's perfect. Make sure they make it under the Christmas tree."

"I still think you should give the gifts to them before you leave."

"Then they wouldn't be Christmas gifts, silly."

"We'll walk you out whenever you are ready." Vinny smiles down at me.

I groan as I realize I forgot to give Christian my work phone back.

I turn the corner and notice the office light is on. I peek inside and see Christian at his desk. Leaning on the door frame, I watch as he runs a hand through his hair and glares at an open folder.

"Shouldn't you be with your wife?"

His icy eyes meet mine. "I was verifying a few items."

"You don't trust us to do your job?"

"I never said that. You're putting words in my mouth, as usual."

"Hopefully good ones." I wink. "And you should be thanking your lucky stars it is just words, after everything you have put me through."

He shakes his head. "Where will I find someone with your spunk and humor?"

"You won't because I'm one in a million."

He stands and stretches. "That you are, Lady Ann, that you are. What can I help you with?"

"I need to give you back my work phone." I offer him the small black cellular device.

"Ann, you should keep it for emergencies."

"Christian, I can't accept this." I push it back towards him.

His blue eyes darken. "I'm your King and you'll accept what I give you, Lady Ann. It's bad enough I have to watch you leave." He rubs his temples. "At least allow me a way to check in on you every now and then."

"Thank you, Christian, you're very kind."

He grabs my arm and pulls me to him. He hugs me tight and kisses my head. I return the hug as I feel fresh tears burning in my eyes. He is a class-A jerk, but I'll miss him.

"I can't imagine my life without you, Ann." He pulls back and looks into my eyes. "Please, stop crying." He runs his thumb down my face.

"I can't help it." I sniff. "You started to get all sappy on me."

"Promise me you'll visit us frequently. And if you don't, I will demand it and make it law." He grabs my chin.

"If you promise to stop calling me Lady Ann." I smirk.

He rolls his eyes. "You're impossible. Just leave me already."

"Just wait until you open your present for Christmas," I throw over my shoulder as I walk towards the stairs.

Once I am out the front door, I breathe in the frigid air.

My eyes scan the entrance for Ryan.

"I'm sure it was too hard for him to say goodbye again, Ann," Karen says as she hugs me.

I look in the rearview mirror and watch the Palace get smaller. My life has changed so much since I first started this adventure. Now I'm returning home with new friends and experiences and I wouldn't change it.

I remember when Ryan drove me home the first time. I was so upset, and I was confident my time at the Palace had ended. I swallow the lump in my throat as I remember that was the turning point for Christian and me. He chose Mary and I was heartbroken.

I swipe at my eyes and stare straight ahead. It is time I woman-up and take charge of my life.

Blizzard

Home at last. I glance up at the brick, three-bedroom, two-bathroom farmhouse. In the corner of my eye, I see our neighbor Suzie walking over and I greet her with a hug.

"Oh, Ann it is so good to see you. Are you finally back home?"

"Yes, ma'am."

"Ryan called and said you would be coming home tonight, so I got the house ready for you. I have some coffee brewing and a casserole in the fridge."

"Thank you, Suzie, would you like to stay and catch up?"

"I wish I could, Ann, but I have an early day tomorrow and it's getting late." She walks back towards her house. "Have a good night, Ann. And welcome home, dear."

I run my fingertips over the glass frames littering the living room walls. Memories of summer days spent in the pool and winter months cuddled in front of the fireplace pass through my mind as I glide over them. I pause at a new picture my dad must have hung up before he left for his trip. I pull it off the wall and hold it tight. It was taken the day of Christian's wedding; everybody was tired and right before the flash, Ryan told a corny joke to ease the mood. A tear falls on the

175

glass and lands over Ryan's grin. As I glance at all the frames, I realize my old life is melding together with this new one.

I find a note by the back door with my dad's chicken-scratch handwriting.

Ann,

When you go out back, do a head count. I think you will be pleasantly surprised at our newest additions. The hidden nest Pecker was monitoring was occupied with fertile eggs and when she fell ill, Fluffy took over. Now we have little Peckers.

All My Love,

Dad

Once I'm outside, my eyes scan the horizon while I scratch my head. I feel a peck on my boot and smirk down at Fluffy. I toss some freeze-dried mealworms at her feet and kneel to stroke her.

"Fluffy, did you raise a flock of Peckers for your sister? Where are they?"

As the other chickens notice the bag of treats, they run at full speed, begging for a taste. I toss a few handfuls and sure enough, strutting over are three black and white roosters that look identical to my sweet Pecker. I swipe at my eyes as I offer them some worms from my open hand.

"Well, now. Dad was right. It looks like we have some new Peckers on the farm. Why don't we stick with the theme and call you Willy, you Johnson, and you Dicky? What do you gentlemen think?"

I laugh at my inappropriate names. Too bad Karen isn't around to enjoy the joke.

Once the treats are gone, I brush my hands off on my jeans.

"Oh, man. It looks like your sister Henrietta is out by the gravestones."

The grass crunches under my boots as I pull my jacket closer. The wind is picking up and the clouds are getting darker.

"Henrietta, you need to strut your fluffy butt right back to the pen, little girl. You don't want to freeze out here, do you?"

The white hen ruffles her feathers and makes her way back towards the pen. I smirk as she pecks the grass as she goes.

I kneel by Pecker's memorial boulder and brush it off gently. The painting Ryan made her is brighter than ever. My eyes burn and I look away as memories flood in.

"Oh, Pecker. I miss you, girl. I hope you and mom are enjoying each other's company. Thank you for the early Christmas gift. Those babies you left are adorable. And I hope they aren't as ornery as you were."

I kick off my boots as I stare at the phone, wondering if I should call and tell everybody I made it home. Should I dial Ryan, Christian, or Karen? I punch in Ryan's number. It rings twice then he answers in his husky voice.

"Hey, Ryan, it's Ann. I was calling to let you, and everyone, know I made it home safe."

"Okay, I'll pass the word along. Have a good night, Ann."

Then the line goes dead.

I frown down at the phone. Well, that was short. I didn't even get to tell him about our newest additions.

I slump into my recliner, next to my bookshelf, and run my finger across the old, worn spines. Oh, how I've missed having time to read. I pull out one of my favorites, lean back, and read for as long as I can keep my eyes open.

The sun rests on my face and I swat it away. I moan as my neck and back protest with pain.

"This is why you don't fall asleep in the chair," I chide myself.

I brave the cold breeze to let the ladies out of their nightly pen. They flock to me, chirping as I pet them and throw food into their feeders. I grumble as I notice that their waters are frozen solid.

I kick the bottom, but that just throws chunks of ice in the air. One piece flings into my eye. I yelp and back up, tripping on Whitey. She runs away, shaking off the attack and warning the others of my betrayal to her backside.

"Sorry, Whitey."

Massaging my hands to get the blood flowing faster, I go to the garage to grab the backup waters. I fill them up with the hope that I can switch out the frozen with the thawed later.

When I walk into the house, the phone is blaring. I kick off my muddy boots and try to run half-frozen to the phone, but I slip and fall. I slap the floor and stare at the ceiling.

Farm life is *so* much fun.

The phone reaches its maximum number of rings, then stops, before I can haul myself back up. Leaning against the counter, I rub my butt. I narrow my eyes at the phone, blaming it for my mishap.

As I go to leave, it rings again and I strangle it.

"Hello!" I blare at the offender.

"Wow, Ann? Is everything okay?" Dan's voice is on the other end.

"My butt is throbbing, and the phone is to blame." I sit on a barstool and cringe.

"That sounds like an interesting story to tell."

"Oh, not as interesting as this call. What's up, Dan?"

"Your dad gave me a call this morning and asked me to come and install some heated waterers for the chicken coop."

I face palm—why hadn't I thought of that?

"That's a wonderful idea, Dan, but you don't have to drive all the way here. I can go run to the store and install them myself."

"Well, it's not that far of a drive, considering I'm sitting in your driveway."

I go to the door as fast as I dare. I open it and see him smirking down at me, wearing jeans and a black leather jacket. I admire him for a minute as he stands there with two heated waterers, one in each hand.

My hero.

"You're a butt-saver. Come inside, Dan."

"Thanks, I guess. I knocked and when no one answered, I tried Ms. Suzie's house, but no one answered there either." He chuckles. "So, I figured I would call until someone picked up."

"You know, I do have a cell phone."

"Oh, I figured that since you left the Palace, you would leave the work phone behind."

"The King insisted I keep it for emergencies." I shrug. "Right this way, Santa. Do you want some coffee before you start?"

"Actually, the weather is supposed to turn nasty soon, so I would rather install it and test it before it gets too bad."

All the chickens look up, curious over Dan and his new equipment. Except for Whitey. She is in the corner, giving me the stink eye as she plots my death.

"You have a lot of beautiful chickens, Ann."

"Thank you. Just don't say that too loudly or you might overinflate their egos." I stroke Henrietta. "Dan, did you say there is severe weather coming?"

"Yeah, your dad called and told me he got a weather alert about a blizzard tonight. He said he meant to install these before he left but it slipped his mind."

He installs the water heaters and turns them on. The chickens cock their heads and peck at them. When nothing happens, they walk away.

The clouds move slowly. I shiver as a breeze kicks up and I hold my jacket tighter against my chest.

"Don't worry, Ann. I'll check around the house and make sure everything is in order before I head out. And your dad said he left plenty of feed inside the garage."

"Dan, you are too good to me."

We watch the water for a little longer, then he pops the lid and puts his finger inside. "Perfect temperature."

"I'm going to arrange some extra bedding and throw corn down for them," I say, looking around the yard and making sure all the hens are accounted for.

"I can help you lift the bedding bags if you want."

"I have been lifting litter bags since I was eight years old. I think I can manage."

"Well, far be it from me to get in the way of your muscle building." He smirks. "I will check out the heater and make sure the pipes are covered."

The ladies peck at the corn and throw the new litter around with their feet, hoping to find more goodies underneath.

"Really, Red? If you keep tossing the bedding, there won't be any for you to snuggle in when the storm comes through."

I walk the property and grab hidden eggs laying around the yard, knowing that they will freeze and explode when the temperature drops.

As I come through the back door, I collide with Dan. I skid to a stop. Then, feeling my boots lose traction, I slip. Before my bruised butt can hit the floor, Dan wraps me in a warm embrace.

We stare into each other's eyes and I swallow. He has amazing emerald-colored eyes and I find myself comparing him to Ryan.

"Ann, are you okay?"

"I think I need new skidproof boots," I laugh as I regain my footing and stand on my own. He holds on a little longer, then he lets go. "Thank you for saving my butt again."

He smirks and walks the other way as I take off my boots and moistened socks.

"So, how about some coffee?"

"Coffee sounds great, thank you. I started the fireplace just in case the heater isn't working great. Plus, the pipes are covered and ready for whatever comes next."

I start the coffee maker and heat up the chicken pot pie casserole Suzie made. I offer him some dinner with his coffee. We sit at the kitchen table, watching the fire crackle over the logs.

At first, there is a blanket of awkward silence surrounding us, but soon I realize we have a lot in common. We talk about chickens, farming, construction, and books. Dan is an avid reader, even more so than I am. And I must admit, it is a turn-on to know a man enjoys reading more than I do.

"I would love to read that FBI, cold case, mystery book you talked about. It sounds intriguing."

"I have it in the truck. Do you want me to get it for you?"

I collect our plates and clean the dishes. When he comes back in, he settles on the couch. I refill our coffee and plop next to him as he fingers through the book, showing me the chapter titles. I run my hand over some writing in the margins.

"What are these?"

"Oh, well. I like to immerse myself in the book. So, I write little notes of what I think may happen, or if I think the author should have done something differently." He blushes.

"Can you read it to me?"

"Me?" he squeaks.

"I find it fascinating the way people read, especially if they are passionate about the book. They add voices and details not spelled out within the pages. Please?" I plead. "If it makes you feel better, we can switch from chapter to chapter."

The fire reflects in his green eyes as he sets his coffee down and accepts my challenge. I snuggle into the couch with a fleece throw and he clears his throat. The book was obviously special to him and his voice was a sweet symphony.

My eyes wander to his mouth as he forms each syllable and I wonder what it would be like to taste his lips.

He abruptly stops and I sit up. Did he just read my thoughts?

"Your turn to read."

I clear my throat, glad he *can't* study my private meditations. I start reading the words slowly at first. Then I pick up my normal pace once I am comfortable. After a while of passing the book back and forth, we are both under the blanket in suspense.

I'm biting my nails when we get lost in the last chapter.

The phone rings and we both yelp. We turn to each other and snicker. I stretch before snuggling back into the couch, not wanting to get up.

"Are you going to get the phone?"

"Nope. If they are important, they can call my cell. Keep reading."

He opens the book as my cell phone buzzes.

"Ann, are you home?" my dad asks.

"Of course, I am, dad. Is everything okay?"

"Yes, I received an alert that the storm is moving in faster than expected and we should be getting one or two feet of snow. The highways are reporting white-out conditions. Make sure you put the ladies up immediately and hunker down. Did Dan check the heater and install the chicken waterers?"

I peek out the front window and gasp. The snow is coming down so hard, I can't see the road or Dan's truck. I feel Dan come up behind me and tense.

"Ann? What was that gasp for?" my dad asks.

"Sorry, dad. Yes, Dan installed all that. He also started the fireplace for me. He is actually still here." I look towards Dan with a smile.

"Thank goodness he didn't leave yet. I was afraid he may have gotten stranded on the highway in this mess. Set up the guest room for him."

Being stuck inside the house—with Dan—that could be dangerous. I glance his way as he observes the snow floating down. I see the flecks dance in his eyes like soft wispy feathers.

"Sure, dad, I'll do that. It is the least I can do after everything he has done for us."

Dan turns to me with a raised eyebrow. I pass him the phone as my dad asks to speak to him.

"What did my dad say?"

"He reminded me to be a gentleman around you, or there would be consequences."

"Dan, I'm sorry. I'm his only daughter and he's a little overprotective."

"He has good reason to be." He brushes a loose strand of my hair behind my ear. Then he turns back to stir the fire.

"So, should we return to the story?"

I jump on the couch and cross my legs. "Yes. And it's your turn."

He gets under the blanket with me and I scoot closer to him. He reads the final chapter, and it leaves the book on a colossal cliff hanger.

"That's not fair. I can't believe they did that."

He laughs as he watches me pout. I grumble as I shove my feet into my boots to put the ladies up.

"Would you like to know what happens next?" He asks as he puts his own boots back on to help me.

"Duh. But the stupid author ruined it."

We gather the girls and check around the yard for stragglers. Once we are sure everybody is tucked inside, we lock the pen and head back indoors. Once we are behind the closed door, we shake the large snowflakes off us.

"Brr!"

"You're grumpy when you are disappointed."

"How can you calmly sit here and tell me you are not mad at that ending?"

"Because I know how it ends."

"How would you know?"

He taps his head. "Because."

"Liar."

"Why would I lie about that? I'm telling you the truth."

"Prove it." I narrow my eyes.

He stomps out of the front door. I run to the front window and try to watch him, but the snow is coming down at all angles as the wind picks up. I bite my lip, worried he may fall or get hurt.

He shivers and shakes off his jacket as I close the door.

"What were you thinking, Dan? There's a blizzard out there."

He grins as he pulls out a brand-new book from his jacket, and I squeal.

"How did you get this copy? The last page said it wouldn't be released for months." I sit on the couch and wrap the warm blanket around me.

"Because I have connections."

How did I not notice this on the first book? I run my hand over the raised letters. "You wrote this?"

He chuckles. "Is it really that big of a shocker?"

"I didn't mean it that way, Dan. I just didn't think you would have had the time... with your job and all."

"I started this one when I was in between projects and needed extra income."

"That is amazing, Dan."

"I know a good publisher if you ever want to write something."

"The only writing I've ever done was for the school paper." I smile at him. "But, thanks, I'll keep that in mind."

We read for a few more hours. Then the power flickers and goes out. I groan as I reach for my phone and turn on its flashlight. I grab some emergency candles from the cupboard and light them.

"So much for the heated waterers for the chickens."

"Don't worry, the water should be pretty warm by now. They'll be fine. Plus, we can fill the other ones tomorrow for them."

"The power probably won't be off long."

The wind howls outside swirling the snow in its path.

"True. Are you ready to call it a night?"

"We can read by candlelight."

"Sounds romantic," he teases as he feeds the blue flames. "We'll need to stay close to the fire until the power comes back on."

I grab blankets and some cushions, tossing them in front of the fireplace as the blower kicks on and starts spewing out hot air. We lie down on the cushions and wrap blankets around us as we use the fire light to read.

During our reading, he pauses and scribbles notes in the margins. It makes me laugh to think he is critiquing his own work. By the end of the book, I can hardly keep my eyes open, but I want to hear what happens.

"That author is pretty amazing. That was definitely a better ending than the first book. He must be enormously proud."

"I believe he is," he says as he sets the book down and yawns. He goes to get up, but I groan and pull him back down.

"You're taking away my warmth."

"We'll freeze if I can't keep this flame going." He feeds the fire a huge log then settles back under the covers with me. "That should be good for a few hours."

He turns to me, but I am already asleep, dreaming about becoming a rebel and fighting the good fight—just like the main character in his book.

In the morning, I hear the heater turn on and the phone ring at the same time. I swat in the direction of the phone. "Stupid, stupid phone."

"Do you want me to grab it, or just let it ring?" Dan says next to me.

My eyes widen as I remember why we are together under the covers. I blink as I notice I am lying on his chest and his arms are wrapped around me. "Uh—sure, if you want to."

He eases out of our makeshift bed and answers the phone.

"Ann, it's for you."

"Tell whomever it is that I'll call them back." Then I turn over and snuggle further under the warm blankets.

"It's Prince Ryan and he doesn't sound like he is willing to let you call him back."

"What is he going to do to me? Spank me? Just hang up." I wave from the covers.

Dan's frown deepens and he goes back to the phone. "She's still waking up. Can she call you back?" He purses his lips at me. "He insists I wake you up and bring you the phone."

I see Dan's forehead glittering with sweat.

"How badly do you want me to get up and get the phone?"

"I'll devote my next novel to you."

I shiver as I pad over to him. "Make sure you spell my name correctly, Dan." Then I turn my attention to Ryan.

"What the hell is Dan doing there?"

"He slept over, Ryan."

Out of the corner of my eye, I see Dan stare at me wide-eyed.

"He did *what*?" Ryan spits out.

"Is there a reason for this early call, Ryan? Other than to give me a headache while I freeze my butt off."

"You are impossible. I called to check on you. I was worried about you. Then I find out that you slept with Dan."

I rub my temple as I glance towards Dan.

"Can you make us some coffee, please? This conversation is taking longer than I expected."

Dan walks over to the coffee machine and bumps his shoulder into mine. "Ann, stop teasing him and just tell him the truth."

"Ann. Explain yourself," Ryan yells.

I hear somebody in the background. Then Ryan pulls away from me and talks to the other person, who in turn grabs the phone from Ryan.

"Ann, how could you sleep with Dan!" Christian yells louder than Ryan had been.

"Oh my gosh. Can you be any louder? I would love for the whole Palace to know about my personal life."

"How dare you do this to Ryan," he blares.

I clench my teeth and hang up the phone. I glare at Dan. "Don't answer that phone."

He laughs as it starts to ring.

"I'm serious, Dan. Do not answer it. I'm going to let the chickens out and check on their water."

Who the heck are they to tell me what to do? Even being hundreds of miles away, they are still trying to run my life.

Freaking control freaks.

I open the chicken pen and the girls flock out. They halt abruptly when they notice the snow. Then they waddle back in to the warmth. I feed them, check their water, and then grab their eggs.

I stroke them softly, wishing I had feathers right now. I walk to the back door, and my boot loses traction on a patch of ice and I am flung to my back.

I open my eyes to see Dan staring at me. "Ann, what happened?"

"I definitely need new boots."

"Ann, your head is bleeding."

I look down and see yellow all around me with a hint of red peppering the snow.

"Oh no! I broke all of their eggs." I sigh as I feel the squishy egg yolks all over me.

"I'm more concerned about the blood, Ann." He wraps an arm around my waist.

"Calm down, Dan. I've survived worse. Remember the hammer?"

He hands me a hot mug as he checks my head. "There's a cut right here." He places a towel with ice in it on my head.

"Ouch." I arch a brow as I listen. "Dan? Am I going crazy, or do you hear voices too?"

He runs to the counter with a curse as he grabs his phone and talks into it.

"They called you on your cell phone, Dan?" I grumble.

"Ann, are you okay?" Ryan asks once Dan presses the receiver to my ear.

I hiss as Dan applies ice. "Yes, perfectly fine, Ryan."

"Dan said you fell down. Then he dropped the phone to help you."

I roll my eyes. "Ryan, as I said I'm—ouch."

Dan presses too hard and I smack him.

"Sorry," he says.

"Ann, are you listening to me?"

"Ryan, I slipped outside because it's icy. It is a part of the farming life. It's no big deal."

"Is there blood?"

"If I say no, will you leave it alone?"

I hear Christian in the background, and he grabs the phone. "Ann, stop being stubborn this instant. Are you bleeding?"

"Not anymore."

"Where did you fall?"

"I already said—outside."

He curses. "I meant what part of your body is bleeding."

"King Christian, you have a country to run, don't you? We just had a natural disaster, and you are worried about me? I think your priorities aren't in the correct place. Go do your job and I'll do mine. I'll be fine, I promise."

"Ann, I'm your King. You can't command me. I'll do what needs to be done."

"Good, so have fun with those reports."

"Ann, please stop hanging up on them. They're going to send the military here in tanks."

I puff out my chest. "They need to remember they have work to do. And that job doesn't include busting my chops."

"They care about you. Can't you just appreciate that and give them the benefit of the doubt?"

"They had their chance! Chances! Let's recall— Christian married Mary and Ryan basically told me that he can't trust me and that he won't have a relationship with me."

"They worry about you, Ann. They may not be able to give you the kind of relationship you want, but at least you have them in your life as friends, right?"

"Doesn't that bother you, Dan?"

"Why would it bother me?"

"Because I know you have feelings for me. But you are pressuring me to keep two guys that I have feelings for as close friends."

"I trust you." He runs a finger along my jawline. "We need to get you out of these clothes." He wrinkles his nose.

I look down, remembering the crushed eggs.

"I can't believe I wasted all those eggs."

He guides me towards my room. "And I can't believe you haven't tossed out those boots yet. Now come on, before the smell gets worse." He watches me pull out clothes. "Are you feeling well enough to shower?

"I may be wounded, but I am not helpless."

I groan as eggshells sprinkle the bathroom floor. I step into the warm water and instantly feel cleaner. I have to scrub the yellow yoke off a few times before it is removed completely. Just as I turn the water off, I hear a bang on the front door. I pop my head out and look around. What the heck was that?

"Dan, is that you?"

I wrap my towel around myself and run out of the door towards the front of the house. I notice Dan standing at the entryway while glaring outside. As I get closer, my mouth drops open when I see Ryan and two Palace guards—Vinny being one of them.

"You son of..." Ryan spits at Dan as he steps forward.

"You don't want to do this. Calm down..." Dan stands tall.

I leap between them, still clutching my towel. "Ryan, what the hell are you doing in Dan's face? Back off!"

"Ann, go put your clothes on." Ryan waves me off.

"This is *my* house. You can't come here barking orders off at me." I turn to Dan. "Dan, please go to my room." When he doesn't move, I ask him again. "Please, Dan?"

Ryan goes to step in his path, but I move faster, blocking his way. "What the hell is wrong with you, Ryan? You are not going to start a cock fight with Dan. Go sit on the couch—you need a time-out!"

Ryan watches Dan's retreating back. "Coward!"

"Vinny, if you are just going to stand there like an idiot, shut the door for Pete's sake!"

"I told you to get dressed."

"This is my house, Ryan! You can't tell me what to do."

His eyes blaze. "How could you?"

"What did I do that is so bad you had to march down here to beat Dan up?"

"You slept with Dan!"

"We slept on the floor in front of the fireplace reading." I motion to the pillows and blankets still sprawled out by the hearth. "See?"

198

He glances in that direction and then steps around me and goes towards my room.

"Ryan, you need to stop right now! You are overreacting and behaving like a bully!"

I squeeze the bridge of my nose, feeling my anger reach its limit.

"Look at me, I am dropping my towel!" All eyes turn to me and I smirk. "Now that I have everyone's attention. Please sit and calm down. Ryan, when I said that Dan and I slept together, I literally meant *slept*, nothing else."

"What?"

I cock a hip. "I am not that kind of girl."

He looks to Dan. "Nothing happened?"

Dan shakes his head and crosses his arms over his chest.

Ryan lets a breath out and rubs his face.

"I am going to make some coffee." Dan says as he brushes past the guards, bumping Vinny with his shoulder.

I sit next to Ryan and put a hand on his leg. "Ryan, how did you get here so fast?"

"I flew."

199

"You flew all the way over here to pick a fight with Dan?"

"Yes. Especially if he did what I thought he did."

"But he didn't. So, maybe you owe him an apology?"

He grumbles incoherently.

"And maybe to me? For barging into my home and trying to hurt one of my guests. Why don't you stay for coffee?"

My eyes land on the jar of black and white feathers Ryan made me when Pecker died. My emotions overtake me and I hug him tightly while I breathe in. He smells so good, like the woods after it rains, and exactly how I remember.

"Ann?"

"Yes, Ryan?"

"What is keeping your towel up?"

I tense and squeeze him tighter, having forgotten my predicament.

"Could you ask the guards to leave for a minute. Just in case my towel falls?"

He nods towards the guards, who in turn shut my door.

"So, which side of you do I get to see?"

I narrow my eyes up at him. I pull back and grab my towel before it falls too far. "None." And I stick my tongue out.

"You are a talented woman, Ann."

I close my bathroom door and throw on my skinny jeans and a white long-sleeved shirt. When I walk out, I see him sitting on my bed and memories of the last time he was here come flooding back.

"Ann, are you feeling okay?"

"My head hurts a little. But I probably just need to eat."

"There is definitely a bump back there."

"Ryan, are you sure you didn't come all this way to say something to me?"

"Nope. I just came to beat Dan up."

I sit next to Dan on the barstool and he offers me a cup of coffee. "Thank you, Dan. I am sorry about Ryan and all of this mess."

Ryan wraps his hand around a mug with a picture of a rose on it. Then he sips it while staring at us. "Dan. Ann said you helped with the chickens?"

"I installed heated waterers for them, checked the pipes and heat for Ann, and started a fire for her."

"They make those?" Ryan asks, tilting his head.

Dan smirks. "Yes, they do."

"Dan also wrote a few books, Ryan." I elbow Dan.

Dan looks to me with an arched brow. Then back to Ryan with a shrug. "Two, so far."

"Can I read them?" Ryan asks.

Dan watches Ryan carefully, unsure if he is teasing him or not. "I am not sure. What is your reading level?"

I spit my coffee out and smack Dan's arm, who then turns to me with humor dancing in his eyes.

Ryan nods as he laughs. "Good one. Though, my reading level has to be better than your coffee."

I breathe a sigh of relief, realizing the tension has left them and they are finally getting along. I lean back in my chair as I watch Dan show Ryan his books and explain their background.

Ryan's cell phone rings and he gets up to take the call. I turn to Dan. "It seems as though you two like each other?"

"Well, we won't be holding hands and skipping together any time soon. But we have common interests." He winks at me.

Then Dan's cell phone rings as well and he excuses himself as he goes to take it. And Ryan comes back. "That was Christian checking in. I updated him and he sends his apologies."

"I would rather have heard it firsthand."

"I bet you would. You love seeing us squirm."

"Not as much as you two relish in keeping me from dating."

Dan comes back in, in a hurry. "Hey, that was your dad. I updated him and he asked me to drive out his way with some of my heavy equipment to help move snow."

"Is he in trouble?"

"No, he just wants to make sure the elderly can get where they need to go. Plus, it's extra money for me and my crew."

"Is it safe out there for you guys? Have the highways opened up?"

"Christian said most of the highways are salted and clear," Ryan chimes in.

"See, I'll be safe." Dan gives me a tight hug. "I will call you later." Then he turns to Ryan. "You can borrow those if you want."

Ryan nods at the books. "Thanks, I will keep them safe for you. And I will spread the word about how good they are." He offers a hand to Dan. "Again, I'm sorry for the misunderstanding."

Dan clasps his hand. "I understand why you did it." He squeezes his palm and narrows his eyes. "Just don't do it again."

I watch him out of the front window as he gets into his truck and carefully drives over the gravel road.

"Wow. Not even a kiss goodbye. Cheapo." Ryan wraps an arm around my neck. "So, he really stayed the night, and nothing happened?"

"Nothing but reading and sleeping. Now let it go, please. Although when I woke up, I was lying on his chest."

Ryan grabs my hand and dramatically places it over his heart. "And here I thought I was the only one to have you sleep on my breasts."

I smack his shoulder, then turn to the kitchen. "Who is hungry?"

Everyone chimes in with a 'yes' and I start cooking a full-course country dinner of chicken and waffles. Ryan assists where he can, but he is pretty helpless in the kitchen, so I send him to set the table and make some sweet tea. Once we all sit down to eat, we start talking about life and I realize how much I miss the Palace, especially the people.

Ryan helps me clear the table. Then I start on the dishes.

"Are you happy here, Ann?"

I stop scrubbing and glance his way. "How can I not be happy with a flock full of Peckers?"

"What?"

"Pecker had babies but they are all roosters and look identical to her. Want to know what I named them? Here's a hint. My choices were borderline inappropriate."

When he doesn't even crack a smile, I frown. "Why do you want to know if I am happy here, Ryan?"

"I was just wondering, that's all."

"Are you happy?"

He shrugs.

"Come on. Talk to me, Ryan."

"I miss you."

"I miss you too, but this is who we are, right? A Prince and a farm girl."

His dark eyes sparkle at mine. "But can't we be more?"

"You said you didn't want a relationship—is that still true?"

He nods slowly.

"Is there any way that Queen Mary will be okay with me returning to the Palace?"

He shakes his head.

"Do you think that Christian will spare you, so you can stay here?"

He shakes his head again.

"Well, I guess we are just going to have to be patient." I stand and walk over to the dishes again.

"What about Dan?" Ryan asks.

"What about him?"

"Are you going to date him?"

I scrub the dish carefully while in thought. "I am not sure."

"Thank you for feeding us, and for not killing me for barging in and trying to murder Dan."

I laugh and pull away from his embrace. "Thank you for the show of muscle. It was entertaining."

He looks into my eyes as he rubs his warm hand down my face. "I am going to miss you."

I kiss his palm. "I will miss you too, but you can call and fly by anytime."

"As much as I would love to, Ann, I think I will give you your space."

I smile as Vinny hugs me goodbye.

"Make sure you give Karen and the baby my love."

"I'll do better than that. I'll replay this day, scene by scene, so she can laugh her butt off at you." He pinches my cheek with a grin. "Our little Ann is being fought over by two men, again."

"You act like I did this on purpose," I grumble as I shove him.

I walk them out and I am amazed to see a small helicopter in our front yard. Ryan climbs into the pilot seat, and I wave slowly as I watch the small aircraft lift off, throwing snow up into the air. I shield my eyes when it creates a snow globe atmosphere all around me.

I repeatedly tell myself that I am a strong independent woman. I don't need *any* man in my life. Heck, I can rule the world without anything holding me back, with just my feathered companions by my side.

But is that really what I want?

Gifts

After Ryan leaves, I vow to stay busy and not mope around the house. So, I call the head librarian, Ms. Stewart, and ask her if they have any openings. She is thrilled over my interest and offers me a temporary position.

The two-story, beige library looms in front of me. I rub my sweaty hands together while I try to convince my feet to move.

"Lady Ann?"

I smile at Ms. Stewart and I offer her a hand with her mounds of books.

"Ms. Stewart, thank you again for this opportunity."

"It is not a problem, dear. It is so wonderful to have you with us. Come this way and I will introduce you to the rest of the team."

After she shows me around and introduces me to the other staff members, she settles me at a desk upstairs.

"This will be your area. You have the computer lab over there. The reading cave over there. And once a week, you will read and do a small craft with the children over here."

"I haven't worked with children before. Are you sure you don't want Margaret doing that?"

"Ann, you are perfect for the job. I saw how you were at the library with King Christian. The children loved you."

"I really don't feel comfortable with this."

She laughs and pats my back.

"Why don't you give it a shot? If you find you can't accomplish it, then we can revisit the idea of handing it over to Margaret. Deal?"

I wring my hands together as I stare at the craft area. Being an only child has always benefited me, until now. I have never been around kids, let alone responsible for teaching them.

What did I get myself into?

"Ann, this isn't a big deal. They are just mini adults."

"Thanks, Dan, you made me feel a hundred times better with that motivational speech."

Dan's laughter bounces off the living room wall as he sets his work down. He grasps my hand and kisses it before I can slap him with it.

"You are a strong woman, Ann. It's one of the many, many traits I admire about you." He runs his thumb over my wrist. "You *can* do this. I know you can."

"I feel as though I have been plucked from everything I understand and thrown into the unknown again. Are you sure you can't come with me tomorrow?"

"I wish I could, but I have to be in the city, bright and early."

I pull my hand away from him and pout.

"I'll do the dishes to make up for it, okay?"

I watch as he soaps the sponge and squeezes. I observe his bicep tighten and I take my eyes away.

"You need to stop pouting over there, Ann, or you will get wrinkles."

My hand flies to my forehead before I stick my tongue out at him.

"Are you going to visit me for Christmas?"

"I wish I could, but I'm staying with my family. It's been a while since I last visited, and they are questioning if I am still alive and well."

"Maybe I could go with you?"

A plate crashes to the floor, sending ceramic shards all over. I jump up to help him.

"Well, I guess that's a solid no, huh?"

"Ann, I would love to take you with me. But I don't want to introduce you to my family right now, especially when you are still in love with Prince Ryan."

"Why would they automatically assume we are a couple? I could go as your friend, Dan."

Dan's face turns red.

"Well, I may have told them about you already. Nothing serious. Just that... well... that I want to date you eventually."

Dan darts past me to throw the broken pieces away, but before he can, I grab his hand and squeeze it.

"Dan, you are the perfect gentlemen, and I appreciate you waiting for me to be ready to date again. But I hate the idea of you sitting and twiddling your thumbs. You should date and bring that special woman to visit with your family for Christmas."

"I don't twiddle, Ann. What the heck is twiddling anyway?"

I move my thumbs around to demonstrate.

"You look absolutely ridiculous. Please stop."

I use my middle finger to show him another trick. His eyes grow wide and he shakes his head.

"That's not very ladylike."

I give him the other hand, brandishing that familiar finger, and smirk.

This sets off a fit of giggles as he throws me over his shoulder.

"That's it, young lady. I'm calling your father and telling him what you just did."

"You can't even bring a woman to your house because you are afraid of judgement. I'm calling your bluff."

Dan sets me on the couch and traps me between his strong arms, his eyes blazing.

I hold my breath while my eyes watch his lips and my body warms. Why can't I get over Ryan faster?

Maybe if I could just have a taste of what Dan has to offer, I could get over Ryan sooner?

Dan pulls me out of my trance when he clears his throat and moves away.

I feel a whimper build in the back of my throat, but I swallow it down. It wouldn't be fair to Dan.

Stupid Ryan. Ruining everything.

"I'm going to pull down the Christmas decorations from the attic before I head out."

Disappointment radiates through my body when he leaves to get the boxes. I was so close. I slump into the couch cushions and place my hands on my hot face.

The next day forty eyeballs watch me as I sway in the rocking chair with a book in my hand. It feels like they are reading my every thought. I swipe my forehead and clear my throat.

"How many of you have ever been so hungry that you ate way too much and got sick?"

The kids stare judgmentally, like I may tell their parents about their crimes of overindulgence.

"I know I have. When King Christian got married, there was an entire table of sweets and I tried everything. That night, I was throwing up rainbows."

They all giggle and nod. I let a breath out and lean back.

"Today we are going to read about a caterpillar that did just that. He eats way too much food and ends up with a stomachache."

I rub my belly for good measure and watch as the kids cross their legs and lean towards me.

While the story plays out, I make noises as if I am eating all the food; and I even pretend my hand is the caterpillar's mouth, chomping on the children with loud 'nom-nom' sounds.

By the end of the event, the kids are laughing and hugging me tightly. I usher them over to the table where they can make their very own caterpillar to bring home.

"Mommy! Lady Ann read to us and helped us make caterpillars! Look at mine. See? I made it with a cat face. Get it? Cat-er-pillar."

The girl waves to me as her mother guides her to the car. I feel a weird sensation pulling at my heart when I watch the kids leave. An empty feeling.

I was going to miss the little monsters. And I look forward to the day when I will eventually have some of my own.

The next few weeks go by quickly as I fall into a routine of taking care of the chickens and volunteering at the library. Every week is a new adventure and I look forward to story time with the kids. We visit a bean stalk, an underwater city, and even a dragon's lair together.

Dan video chats with me, giving me updates on his jobs, while Ryan does what he promised and gives me my space. Karen calls near the end of the week to inform me that her and Vinny will be moving to their new home. I offer to help them move, but they have already paid a company to do it; however, they do accept my offer for dinner, once they have settled.

When I get off the phone, I lean back in my recliner. Christmas was fast upon us. I look around the bare house. I hadn't put the decorations up, because I had been too busy to celebrate. But now that the library didn't need me, because of a lack of funding, I had little to do to keep my mind busy.

The sting of loneliness brings my knees to my chest. I cry softly—missing Karen, my dad, Dan, and most of all, Ryan. His face swims in my memories, and his laugh echoes through my heart before I drift off to sleep.

The next day the doorbell pulls me away from my morning chores.

"Don't worry, girls, I'll be right back."

I toss some corn over my shoulder as I rush to open the door. My breath is pushed out of me as my dad grabs me in a hug.

"Surprise! Merry Christmas, Ann!"

I blink up at my dad's dorky grin.

"Dad, don't you have a key? Why did you knock?"

His chuckle rings through the house.

"No hi or hug for your old man?"

I wrap my arms around him.

"Welcome back, dad. I missed you so much."

"Now, that's more like it. I drove through the night to make it here in time."

His disappointment is palpable as his eyes scan the house.

"Did Dan forget to grab the decorations from the attic before he left?"

"Dan did grab them down for me, but I have been so busy with the library and chores that I haven't had time to put them up." I shove a box into his hand. "But now that you are here, we can do it together."

His eyes sparkle while a grin spreads across his face.

"That's a great idea, sweetie! I'll put some Christmas music on and make some hot chocolate. I know, I know. You want extra marshmallows with two packets of chocolate with yours. I may be old, but I still remember what my little girl likes."

My dad ruffles my hair when he brushes past me, humming "Jingle Bells."

The music is contagious and makes my heart swell. Who needs a boyfriend when you have the best dad in the world?

After we decorate the house, I make my mom a gift.

"Ann, that is beautiful."

I hold the homemade wreath close to my heart as we walk towards mom's headstone.

"Dad, do you think mom can see us?"

"Of course, she can, sweetheart. And I know she is as proud of you as I am."

"What have I accomplished? I'm twenty-two years old with nothing to show for myself."

"Don't shortchange yourself, Ann. Plus, you are never too old to start scratching things off a bucket list. You are the master of your life, Ann. If you aren't happy with it, get up and do something about it, because feeling sorry for yourself will only hinder your greatness and you won't accomplish anything."

We kneel at my mom's headstone and fall silent, lost in our own emotions.

"AnnaBelle, we miss you. Merry Christmas, my love."

My dad leans forward and sets a kiss on the picture of my mom's beautiful face. Then he swipes his eyes and lays the wreath over it. The long red ribbon flutters in the wind.

I wrap an arm around his waist.

"When I die, I want to be placed right next to her," I say softly, as tears take over my vision.

"Don't talk like that, Ann. You are far too young to even be thinking about your end. Plus, I get to lay next to her since I'm going first."

"Hey, I don't want to think about you leaving me to fend for myself."

He chuckles and kisses the top of my head.

"Fine. We will die on the same exact day and time. Deal?"

"Do you promise?"

The silence among us thickens as the cold night air passes over us.

"I promise, sweetie."

"You know if you lie to me, you will go to Hell."

We both laugh as we wipe our tears away.

That night the fire detector goes off inside the house as I close the chickens up.

"Dad?" I call through the thick smoke.

"Damnit! I can't believe I burnt the ham." My dad coughs as he waves a potholder at the blaring alarm.

I help him divert the smoke until the alarms cease their screeching assault.

"Dad, I told you I would have cooked it."

My dad slams down the potholders, making me jump.

My eyes grow wide as I realize he forgot to turn the burner off. I yelp as red flames appear behind his back.

I slam a cookie sheet full of decorated sugar cookies on top of the flames, until the fire alarms are going off again, but at least the fire is out.

The disaster of the kitchen takes my breath away. I turn to my dad to make a joke, but my words fail me.

"Dad, it's okay. We can make something else for dinner."

"I wanted to make this Christmas special for you. And I failed miserably."

Dad plops on the barstool and shakes his head.

I grab a sugar cookie off the floor and take a bite.

"Hey, we still have the five-second rule, right?"

"Ann, don't eat off the floor."

I shove the whole cookie in my mouth and smirk at him with chipmunk cheeks. I feel the mood shift, and I know I have accomplished my goal.

"Dad, talk to me. What's really going on?"

"I know it's only a matter of time before you and Ryan get back together and get married. You won't need me anymore."

I let his words wash over me.

"Dad, I will always need you in my life."

He grunts and looks around the smoke-filled room.

"Okay, so I might not need you to help me cook, but what about decorating the house? Or building a chicken coop? I love you, dad. You will always be the number one man in my life."

I tap my shoulder on his.

"Ryan doesn't want me back, dad, so all this worrying is over nothing. Now, pull yourself up by those bootstraps and let's cook some edible food before

Karen and Vinny get here. Because you know if they see this disaster, they will never let us live it down."

We start stew and biscuits as Karen and Vinny pull up.

I grin down at Karen's pregnant belly.

"Oh, my goodness! Look at you, girl! It has been far too long." I laugh and rub her belly.

She rolls her eyes. "Ann, stop petting me like an animal. I feel like I am a ginormous tank."

I offer her a seat at the table while Vinny helps dad bring in the goodies. The stew, biscuits, salad, and sweet tea decorate the red tablecloth.

"So, how is the new house coming along?"

"It's going great. I am excited to get unpacked and start this new chapter in our lives," Karen says as she grabs Vinny's hand.

Vinny pokes at his food quietly.

"Vinny, is something wrong with the stew?" I frown.

He forces a smile. "No, it's delicious. Thank you. I just miss my job at the Palace, that's all."

I nod. "I miss the Palace too, if it makes you feel any better. I thought coming here would make me happy but I just... I miss... things."

"He misses you too," Karen says softly.

"Who?"

"Ryan. He is immersing himself in his work and always walking around with a frown. And when he unwrapped your Christmas gift, he just seemed to close off even more."

"Really?"

"Yeah, he is like a pitiful lost puppy dog."

I clear my throat and change the subject as I feel tears prick my eyes.

"Vinny, can you still work at the Palace from here?"

"It is too long of a drive."

"I am sure there is a security place here that would love to have you."

Karen stands up abruptly, causing her chair to tumble to the floor. "You should have told me this wasn't what you wanted before we moved here!"

He watches her carefully. "Not now, Karen."

"Yes, now! We bought the property, built the house, and now you have changed your mind!"

"I didn't want to upset you and ruin your dreams!"

"Well, too late!" She throws her napkin down and goes to the bathroom.

I stand to go to her, but Vinny lifts a hand, stopping me. "Just give her a minute. She hates having people witness her cry. These hormones make her a little emotional. Then she gets embarrassed... it is a vicious cycle."

"It's not too late. You guys can sell the house and move closer to the Palace."

"It's not that we don't like the house. I just want to work at the Palace. I was needed there, you know?"

"I know what you mean, Vinny. I love this farm life, but without Ryan, it feels empty." I wrap my arms around myself.

"Have you told Ryan that?"

"Why would I tell him that? He has made it clear that he doesn't want me."

"You should explain to him how you feel."

Karen sits down and lets out a breath. "I am sorry everyone. I tend to be a little sensitive lately."

I rub her back. "It is understandable, little sister."

She turns to Vinny. "I love you, Vin Bear. Wherever you want to go, I will be there. Even if that means moving back to the Palace."

The Christmas tree twinkles and glitters in the corner of the room. Having my friends and dad surrounding me for Christmas is exactly what I need.

I glance towards Karen's phone as she scrolls through her ultrasound pictures. Although to me, it looks like an ugly alien growing inside her, she is over-the-moon happy.

"The baby looks like a pair of butt cheeks to me."

"Ann, that's because we are having twins!"

"So, they will be born looking like your rear end?"

"Stop it! They are cute little peanuts. Can't you see them? Look. Here is one baby. Then, right here, is another."

I shove the phone back into her hand.

"No matter how long I look at it, I will never see it." I squeeze her. "As long as they don't come out looking like your butt and are healthy, I'm happy for you guys."

"I'm never showing you my ultrasound pictures again. Calling my children butt cheeks."

"Stop pouting. You can't tell me they look like babies either."

My dad tosses us gifts and wrapping paper goes flying.

"Dad! This is perfect!"

I rub my finger across the necklace with a little black feather dangling from it.

"You are most welcome and thank you for the watch, sweetie."

"I even had your name inscribed on the back, dad."

We look over the watch, and it makes my heart sing when he clicks it into place on his wrist.

"And you better believe I am going to use this Spa gift certificate ASAP! We should go together!"

"I'm not a big Spa person, Karen. You go and enjoy yourself." I turn to Vinny. "I wasn't sure what to get you. I hope you can use that."

"Are you kidding? This gift card to Guns R Us is perfect. They have all kinds of manly items there."

I hug them both before watching them drive away.

"Well, I need to be off too, Ann."

"Thank you for a great Christmas, dad. I love you. Drive safe."

"I love you too, Ann. I'll call you soon."

After he pulls away, I close the door to sit and read before bed, but the words don't make sense. I rub my eyes and sigh, looking down at my phone. I tap on an app and run a hand through my hair as I stare at the video chat, waiting for it to connect.

"Ann? Is everything all right?"

"Why do you assume something is wrong, Dan?"

"Because your dad was cooking for you." He chuckles.

"I had the fire extinguisher ready."

I squint at the grey and dreary background. Then I hear a male voice ask Dan who he is talking to.

"Well, my brother is calling for me, Ann. We are getting ready to eat." He moves away from the loud voice while waving his hand at the figure. "I'm coming! Give me a second, you idiot."

I feel my lips pull into a grin. What would it have been like growing up with a sibling? Would we get along?

"Merry Christmas, Ann. I'll keep in touch. Have a good night."

"What, you aren't going to introduce me to your brother?" I smirk.

"Uh, no."

I hear the male voice declare, claiming that he is cuter and that's why Dan won't share me with him. I roll my eyes as their argument—over who's better—gets heated.

"Go whoop his butt, Dan. I'll talk to you soon. Merry Christmas, to you both."

"Thank you, Ann. Don't forget to check under your tree. I sent you a little something."

"I was going to wait until you came back to open it."

"Trust me on this one, Ann. You'll want to open this sooner rather than later. It is time-sensitive."

I jump off the couch and grab the manilla envelope, with my name on it, out from under the tree.

"Speaking of gifts, where is the hat I got you?"

"Safe in my truck, away from my condescending brother."

I chuckle as I imagine him wearing the custom hat I bought him—that said 'Dan the Man' with a toolbox—in front of his brother.

I rip open my gift and grin.

"It's your manuscript for your third book. Thank you, Dan."

"I hope you like it."

"I am sure I will love it, Dan. I'll make my corrections and give it back to you."

He laughs. "I wouldn't expect anything less from you, Ann. Good night."

I press the end button and lean back. I flip through his manuscript with my red pen in hand. It is going to be a long night and I can't wait.

Help is on the Way

The next morning, while I start my coffee, my cell phone rings.

"Ann, it's Tim. How are you doing?"

"I am doing well. How are you doing, Tim? How is the boyfriend?"

"Oh, he is great. He bought me an ugly turtleneck for Christmas just so we could argue and make out."

"Well, I am glad you had a productive Christmas."

"That I did, and how was yours?"

"It was great. My dad, Karen, and Vinny came over. Oh, and Karen told me she is having twins! Can you imagine that?"

"Oh, wow! No kidding? Twins? They are going to have their hands full. I'm glad you had a great Christmas."

"Thank you. So, Tim, what can I do for you?"

"The King asked me to call and see if you could possibly come to the Palace for a few days. Everyone has fallen ill due to the Flu and he needs help desperately."

"The Flu?"

I remember hearing the news talk about it being unbelievably terrible this year. A lot of people are catching it, and some have even lost their lives.

"Ryan is the only one who hasn't fallen sick yet and he is working himself to the bone. Ann, you know the office and how the King likes it ran. Could you come and help us out? The King has offered to pay you and, of course, to house you in your original room."

"That is very generous of him." I run my hands through my hair. "Of course, I will come, Tim. I will set things up here and be there before nightfall."

"Thank you, Ann! He will be thrilled. See you soon."

Did I just agree to go back? I bang my head on the wall. What was I thinking?

I was thinking they need help, and I am it. I dial dad, Suzie, and Karen and update them on the situation. Suzie offers to watch the chickens for me, and I thank her for her generosity. Then I work on packing some comfortable clothes and necessities.

I check on the chickens and the house before getting into the car and starting the long drive. I stare ahead, thinking about how horrible it must be for the entire family to be sick.

I better keep my hands clean.

When I get to the Palace gate, I am greeted warmly by the guards, who recognize me immediately. I park in the garage and come in through a side door, making my way up towards the third floor with my bag. When I reach my destination, I pop my head into the office to find Tim. He looks up and jumps to his feet to hug me.

"Ann! It has been too long."

"Tim, you look great."

"I do, don't I?" He winks.

"I am going to set my bag in my room and then get started."

I open the door and glance around. It looks the same as before I left. I turn the lights on and throw my bag on the bed. I stop short in the hallway as I spot Ryan.

My heart races and I feel my palms moisten. I watch as he glances down at some papers and his dark hair falls over his eyes. He needs a haircut badly. I take in his black dress pants and baby blue button-up shirt. He glides his hands through his hair then glances up. When our eyes meet, he rubs his lids and blinks.

"Did you miss me?"

He holds me tightly, like I might turn and run. Then he pulls back and stares at me. "Ann? What are you doing here?" He looks me up and down.

"Tim called and asked for back-up."

"Why? I am taking care of everything."

I move my fingertips to a loose strand of hair by his eye. I tuck it back and smile. "Stop being stubborn and tell me what I can do to help."

I grab his arm and his eyes light up.

Together, we go through reports and make phone calls, constantly bumping into each other in Christian's small office.

Tim knocks on the door and I wave him over.

"Can I get you two something to eat?"

"Thank you, Tim. Yes, I am starving." I turn to Ryan, who is glaring at a piece of paper while communicating on the phone. "Surprise us with something quick and tasty."

I lean on the doorframe, observing Ryan. When he catches my gaze, he pauses and drops his pencil. I laugh as it rolls off the desk and onto the floor. I hand it to him, and he returns his scowl to the phone.

I missed him so much and I know I won't be happy leaving this time.

Tim comes in with sandwiches and fries. After a few minutes of watching him ignore it, I walk to Ryan with my hands on my hips. He glances at me then away. I take the sandwich and shove it in his face but he waves me off.

I kneel in front of him with my hand outstretched. When he rolls his eyes, I gently grab the phone from him. I point to his food, forcing him to eat as I finish the phone call.

"I understand your situation, sir, but we really need those medications delivered as soon as possible. No, that timeframe is unacceptable. Of course. We understand. Thank you for your help, we'll see you soon." I hang up the phone and sit in the chair before taking a bite of my sandwich. When I glance up, I see Ryan gawking at me. "What? Did I dribble mayonnaise on my shirt?"

"I was on the phone with that jerk for twenty minutes and nothing! Then you waltz in here and get him to agree, just like that!"

"Ryan, you are over-exaggerating."

He tosses a pickle at me. I gasp and throw it back. Then he chucks a tomato. I go to throw it back as well but stop mid-release as Mary saunters in.

The tomato and pickle fall to the floor. We look up at her scowling face.

"Lady Ann, what are you doing back at the Palace so soon?"

"Christian asked me to help while everyone is sick with the Flu."

Her eyes throw daggers at Ryan. "Did you invite her here?"

Ryan shakes his head as he bites into his sandwich.

"I told you, Christian invited me."

"I'm sorry, but we don't need your assistance."

I cross my arms over my chest. This girl has some nerve. I drove all the way here, and she is trying to toss me out already.

"Where have you been all day while I have been in here working?"

"My husband is ill, so I am taking care of him."

"You have nurses and doctors for that," I retort.

"Get out!" she hisses.

I stand and glare at her as I hear everyone in the office go silent.

Ryan finishes his sandwich and stands as well. "Mary, she is here to stay and help."

"No, she isn't needed." She crosses her arms over her chest.

I shake my head and push past her to grab my stuff.

"Ann, wait! Please, don't go!" Ryan calls out to me. I grab my bag and turn to him in my doorway. "Please."

My eyes run over Ryan. The poor guy needed a good night's rest and a shower. How could I let Mary get under my skin so easily? I must be losing my edge.

"You are right. I am here for you and Christian, *not* her."

He opens his arms and I run to him as he holds me close to his chest. "Never leave me," he whispers into my hair.

I squeeze him, unable to make that promise, knowing Mary held more power than he did, and I wasn't sure how long this was going to last.

We return to the office, hand in hand.

"Ann, I thought you were leaving?" Mary huffs.

"I'm sorry to disappoint you, Mary. But I take my orders from the King and Prince and so far, neither has asked me to leave."

"I am the Queen and what I say goes. Guards, I demand you escort her out immediately!"

The guards look to me then to their Queen, but they do not move. Mary's face turns red as she stomps towards me with balled fists.

One of the bedroom doors opens and Christian pops a pale face out of it.

"You three need to come with me now," he says slowly.

We all move into the dark room as he sits back on the edge of the bed, hunched over. I help him get under the covers and he smiles up at me. "Thank you, Ann, for coming to assist us. It hasn't been the same around here since you left."

"I bet it has been much quieter, huh? Why did you ask me here, Christian?"

"We need assistance right now and I had no choice but to call you back."

Mary pales. "But Christian I thought we agreed…"

"Mary, I'm your husband, but your King first and foremost. And as your leader, I'm severely disappointed at the way you have treated a Palace guest. Ann is welcome here anytime. And as of now, and until I say otherwise, she holds higher power than you. Since obviously, you have allowed your power to go straight to your head."

I turn my smug look towards Christian. "Are you okay?"

He laughs weakly. "Do I look okay?"

"Are you sure this is only the Flu?"

He nods. "It has been going around the country like wildfire. Mom got it first and seems to be doing better. So, I should be good in a few days."

"Well, don't worry about the office work, Ryan and I are handling it. You just concentrate on getting better."

He squeezes my hand. "Thank you again. Don't let anyone stop you from coming back, do you hear me?"

When the doctor enters to check on Christian, Ryan and I return to the office. After a while, Tim pops his head in. "So, I hear we have a new Queen around here?"

I look up from my papers and rub my temples. "Tim, please don't start."

"I'm sorry, but I do need Her Majesty to sign these forms for me."

I turn to Ryan who is smirking at me. "What?"

"Oh, nothing. I'm just remembering the look on Mary's face when you told her no. Then when the guards didn't listen to her. Then again when Christian told her you were higher on the food chain than her. Priceless."

"Where did that pickle go?" I look around for something to throw at him.

"It's good to have you back, Ann. You seem to always bring drama wherever you go."

I throw my pen at him. "That's not fair! I do not."

"Hey. It makes my life more interesting."

"Well, I always aim to please." I narrow my eyes.

After work, we leave the office and head towards our rooms.

Ryan ushers me inside his room. "I finally got a chance to read Dan's books before the Flu epidemic hit. And I agree with you. The books are pretty amazing."

"Dan definitely is a talented writer. The imagination and creativity of his worlds are very captivating."

"You can give the books back to him the next time you see him." He hands them to me. "Are you going to be seeing him soon?"

"I'll hold on to them for him. But I'm not sure when I'll be seeing him again."

"So, you two aren't together?"

"No. Just calling each other on the phone every now and then."

Ryan gently grabs my arm.

"I didn't mean to upset you."

"Ryan, what is it you expect from me?"

He watches my eyes before he scans down to my lips. Then he grabs my waist and pulls me closer to him.

"I expect you to always be close to me. So, I can do this whenever I choose to."

He lowers his warm lips to mine, sending a jolt of passion through my body. My arms wrap around his neck as he deepens the kiss. It is hard to breathe as he seems relentless—both needing to have me and afraid of letting me go.

Hesitantly I pull back, "Ryan, I can't breathe." I gulp in air. "I can barely stand."

He rests his forehead on mine. "I am glad I have some power too." I roll my eyes but lay my ear on his strong chest. "Ann, I have missed you so much. Please come back to me. I'm done guarding my heart. It is all yours."

My heart soars as his words soak into my weary soul.

"Ryan, are you sure?"

"Yes, as long as you will have me." Then he shrugs. "I mean Dan is pretty amazing."

"He is pretty amazing, but not as amazing as you."

When I wipe my tears, he smiles at me. "Ann, can I kiss you again?"

"You better, if you want me to stay around."

We become entangled again in a passionate embrace. It felt so good to be back in his arms.

"We should probably get some sleep."

"Are we sleeping in your room or mine?" I say against the soft flesh on his neck.

He groans lightly. "Both, let me escort you to yours."

"Just remember, I have the power to tell you what to do," I tease as we walk.

"Oh, I look forward to it."

As we arrive at my room, we turn to see the doctor running into Christian's. We both turn to each other with arched brows then go towards where he entered.

"Doctor, is everything okay with Christian?" Ryan speaks up.

"Prince Ryan, your brother has spiked another fever and he is dehydrated. So, we are giving him an IV with fluids and a fever reducer."

I grab Christian's palm. "We are here, Christian. Don't worry about anything, just get better."

When he weakly squeezes my closed palm, I kiss his fingertips gently.

In like, Ryan grabs his other hand and says, "I finally asked Ann out, big brother. So, you can stop pretending to be sick to get us back together."

Christian replies with a shake of his head.

Mary dabs Christian's forehead with a wet cloth as a tear rolls down her painted face.

"Mary, I am sure Christian will be fine."

She looks up, her blue eyes glittering. "Ann, about earlier…"

"It's fine. You are stressed, and your husband is sick. I understand."

When we return to my room, Ryan sits on my bed and stares at the wall.

"Ann, I am worried about Christian."

"Of course, you are, Ryan." I lean my head on his shoulder. "But he is strong. He will make it."

He runs a hand down my face. "I am sorry I wasted so much time."

"You were just playing hard to get," I tease.

"I love you, Ann."

My heart swells to the point of bursting. "I love you too, Ryan."

Then he closes my door softly.

That night, my heart is filled with love, and I sleep with dreams of what the future may hold.

I hear a knock at my door and someone whispering softly. At first, I think I am dreaming.

"Mary, is everything all right?"

"Christian is asking for you."

I get up and throw a robe on over my silk lavender nightgown. Mary stands outside the door as I walk in.

"Aren't you coming in too?"

239

"He asked for a private conversation."

"Christian?"

I stop dead in my tracks. His face is pale, his blue eyes dim, and he has dark circles under his eyes.

"Stop looking at me like that, Ann."

"Like what?" I tilt my head, letting my chestnut locks fall over my shoulder.

"Like you may never see me again."

"That would never happen. Christian, you are far too stubborn to leave someone else in charge."

He laughs weakly then coughs. I offer him some water. "You are absolutely right. But, Ann, if something does happen to me… I need you to promise me you will be here for Ryan."

"Well, I don't expect you to go before me. So, it doesn't matter," I say as I raise my chin. "I mean, honestly, a pair of heels almost killed me. Then a hammer. The odds are not in my favor."

"Oh, Ann, I missed that humor and spunk," he says as he leans back against his pillow. "Promise me that you will stay and help him."

"You know I will." I sigh. "I promise." I look down at his hand, then to his face. "He told me he loved me."

"Finally." He chuckles. "He can be so daft at times."

"Yeah, just like someone else I know. Hey, why don't I read the financial report to you? Maybe you just need some mental stimulation to help you ease into better health?"

I swipe at my eyes, not sure what else to say to move away from the topic.

"If not, I am sure it will help me sleep, right?"

I grab the recent financial report and as I turn to leave, I fight back tears. Christian can't die. With all the doctors and medical supplies, surely, they can get him back to health?

I walk to his room and smile as I see Mary back inside, dabbing his forehead. I sit next to her, open the report, and read. He listens and even inputs corrections. I continue reading until I see the sun peeking through his curtains. I open them, letting the sunshine in. Christian groans and closes his eyes.

"Christian, you need more vitamin D. No more of this doom and gloom."

Mary giggles as Christian covers his face. There is a knock, and the doctor comes inside to check on Christian.

Ryan walks out of his room as I leave Christian's, and he arches a brow. "Ann, are you still in your pajamas?"

"Don't start with me, Ryan. Your brother woke me up thinking he was dying. It has been a rough night."

"Really? I am sorry, Ann."

"Are you feeling all right, Ryan? You are looking pale."

"I am fine, just ready for my vacation."

"Are you still planning on going?"

"Why not?"

"Well, a lot has changed since you said you wanted to see the country."

"You are still welcome to come with me."

"Maybe I will… after all this is over."

I eye my bed eagerly, wishing I could take a quick nap and catch up on my sleep, but I know I shouldn't leave Ryan to take care of everything on his own. So, I change quickly before I go towards Christian's desk and get busy. By the end of the day, I lean back, ready to crash. I close my eyes and raise my hands to the heavens.

"Thank God! It feels good to be caught up, huh?" I ask Ryan.

"Yes, it does. Ann, I couldn't have done this without your help. This blizzard really turned everything upside down. But we pulled through it."

I put a hand on his forehead.

"Ryan, you are hot."

"I know." He winks at me.

"Come on, sicko. Before you spread this awful virus any further and we lose our entire workforce. Let's get you to bed and have the doctor look at you."

"But I don't want to."

When we get to his room, I help him under the black down comforter. Then I ask his butler to get some soup and bread while I call for the doctor. When the doctor arrives, he takes some blood samples, and checks his blood pressure and his temperature.

"Looks like you will be bedridden for a few days, Ryan. Until this fever goes away. We don't want to keep spreading this virus around." He glances towards me. "You might want to keep your distance."

"Too late, doc, I have been exposed." I wink at Ryan.

We eat our chicken noodle soup and then I tuck Ryan in.

"Ann, can you sit with me until I fall asleep?"

I kiss his hot forehead. "Let me go update your brother and I will be right back."

When I enter, I am surprised to see Christian sitting up and eating. I smirk at him. "So, I guess you are not dying after all?"

"Sorry to disappoint you, Ann."

"Well, it seems you have spread it to your brother. He is bedridden and requires my full attention."

"I was hopeful it was going to pass over him. I should be ready to return to the office soon."

"I am glad you are feeling better, Christian. We just got caught up from the blizzard storm madness. Which I'm working on renaming to Mary 2.0. And now it is only the regular day to day stuff, with the Flu epidemic sprinkled in."

"I need to do a press release. The Flu is spreading very quickly. I should go over hygiene and aftercare instructions..."

I place a hand on his. "You need to recover first and get some rest. Do you want me to do the report?"

"You're willing to go in front of a group of reporters?"

"If that is what you need me to do... to keep your stubborn butt from doing too much."

"I appreciate it, but it has been a while since I have made an appearance. They may start to worry if they don't see me soon." He squeezes Mary's hand next to him and she stirs in her sleep. "Poor thing, she hasn't slept well in days." He smiles at her sleeping figure. "Go take care of Ryan and get some rest. Mom's quarantine is up tomorrow so she will be in the office. And if all goes well, mine will be over tomorrow night."

When I enter Ryan's room, I watch his chest rise slow and even. I smile as I run my hand through his hair, gently admiring his soft dark locks. Then I kiss his feverish head and slip into bed beside him.

Throughout the night, I keep a cold rag nearby to dab on his forehead and water bedside for him to drink, so he doesn't get dehydrated. His feverish slumber is restless, and I get little rest myself. When morning comes, the doctor returns to check on him. "Well, it looks like his fever has broken."

"That was quick."

"In all the time I have taken care of the Prince's health, he has always had a strong immune system. Just keep an eye on him and let me know if the fever spikes again. If it doesn't, he should be able to leave his room tomorrow." Then he walks out.

Ryan stares into my eyes. "Am I dreaming, or are you really in my bed in a flimsy nightgown?"

"Yes, you are dreaming."

He pulls me close. Then he trails warm kisses over my neck slowly. "If I am really dreaming, I should take advantage of this situation."

After he kisses my neck, he sighs into my hair and falls back to sleep. Then I drift off to sleep myself, comfortable in his strong arms.

When I wake up, I pat the empty bed.

"Ryan?"

He pokes his head out of the bathroom with wet hair and water dripping down his face. "Yes?"

"I'm just making sure you didn't run away."

He walks out with a towel draped over his waist. My mouth goes dry as I stare at his sculpted chest and arms. He leans towards me. "Do you have something to say to me?"

"Not particularly."

He dips his lips close to mine, and the heat radiating off his chest reflects the warmth of my body. His lips touch mine in a passionate embrace and his hands run through my hair. When he pulls away, my lips are swollen, and my face is flushed.

"Ryan, stop it or I am going down next."

"You are too stubborn for that."

I sneak out of the room to grab clothes and collide with my dad in the hallway. "Dad?" I throw my arms around him as he laughs.

246

"I just left your room and I was heading to the office to see if you were in there." He quirks a brow. "Were you sleeping in Ryan's room?"

I open and close my mouth, feeling like I am ten years old again and getting caught with my hands in the cookie jar. Ryan walks out just in time to save me from myself.

"Jack, what are you doing here? I would hug you, but I am still on quarantine."

"Is there something you want to tell me?"

"Welcome back?" Ryan grabs me. "Oh, and your daughter and I are together."

"You better be good to my daughter, because even if you are a Prince, I won't hesitate to give you a piece of my mind if you hurt her." My dad chuckles and turns to me. "Ann, can we talk?"

"Of course." I lead him into my room as Ryan sneaks back into his own. "Are you okay, dad?"

"Yes, I just came by to check on my daughter. This Flu epidemic is crazy."

"I agree. Elizabeth just got off quarantine, Christian's ends tonight, and Ryan's ends tomorrow. As long as the fevers do not come back."

"And what about you?"

"I feel fine. How about you?"

"I'm healthy as a horse."

"How are your travels going?"

"Good. I am still traveling and working on something for Elizabeth."

"Dad, you aren't still looking into Mary, are you?"

"I'm just poking around in her hometown while working on some projects here and there."

"Dad, please drop it. Mary is our Queen now and Christian's wife. If he trusts her, so should you."

"But, Ann, something does not feel right about her."

I lay a hand on his. "Daddy, please, let it go and just enjoy your retirement, okay?"

"Enough about me, what about you? Specifically, you and Ryan?"

"We know we love each other. So that's a start."

"Of course, you two love each other. You have just been too stubborn to acknowledge that."

"Me!"

"Sorry, both of you." He smirks.

I roll my eyes. "No, just him."

"How about we get something to eat?"

"How about you catch up with Elizabeth while I change? I will meet you in the office."

He nods as we hug. "I love you, Ann. I am so happy for you."

"Thanks, dad, now go before you make me cry."

I watch his departing figure and frown. He was hiding something from me. I sigh and acknowledge that I need to talk to Christian to see if we can catch my dad up on Mary's situation. That way, my dad will stop his fruitless searching.

I pull out a simple purple sundress and flats. I apply some light makeup and brush my hair. When I enter the office, I notice Snowball strutting around as if she owns the place. I giggle at her until I spot my dad chatting with Elizabeth, and my heart soars. Maybe that's what he is hiding? Maybe they have something going on?

After everyone is off their quarantine, we all sit in the dining room while our glazed ham is served.

"Jack, it is wonderful to see you again." Christian shakes his hand.

"Thank you, King Christian."

"And mother, I noticed white feathers on my desk. Now that I am returning to work, please keep your animal restrained."

"Aw, Christian did Snowball leave you a tiny gift on your desk?" I elbow him.

"Lady Ann, this is hardly the time or place to be conversing about such topics." Mary side glances me.

Ryan grins as he whispers into my ear. "You know. Christian never revoked your power. So technically, you are more influential than Mary. I dare you to tell her to shut it."

Mary clears her throat. "Prince Ryan, why are you whispering? Speak up so that we may all hear your conversation."

"I'm sorry, but I can't—it's *inappropriate*." He smirks at Mary.

"Well, I'll make an exception this time. Please tell us what couldn't have waited another moment."

"I was telling Ann about the *real* gift that Snowball gave Christian— when he changed her diaper."

I choke on my mashed potatoes then my eyes shoot to Christian's beet red face.

"This discussion is over." Christian clears his throat.

Ryan leans in to whisper again, but when he catches Mary's glare, he speaks loudly instead. "Christian must have had a *crappy* day."

I burst out laughing—holding onto my sides. Once I catch my breath, I fist bump Ryan.

After dinner, I bowl with my dad at the Palace's bowling alley. Then I make my way to Ryan's room. I knock and peek inside. I watch as he sits behind his desk with his sketchpad. I enter unnoticed as he draws a design of a building. I tilt my head while he draws lines and makes measurements. "That's beautiful, Ryan."

"It isn't done yet. I am just starting the design." He admires his work. "I was inspired."

"What is it for?"

He makes a few more lines with his ruler. "It is a house."

"That sounds nice. Who are you making it for?"

"I am making it for us."

I quirk a brow. "Us?"

"Well, I mean one day… in the far future of course." His cheeks pinken.

I look down and see the high arches, two spacious bedrooms, and a large master.

"Are you planning on us having two kids?"

"Well. I assume. Maybe one day," he stutters. "If not, I can have a room to use as a studio, and you can have the other for a photo gallery."

I kiss the top of his head. "You are very thoughtful."

He lets a breath out.

I continue to sit with him as he draws. The silence is comforting as I watch him plan out our future.

"Do you still intend to go on your trip around the world?"

"Only if you will accompany me. I don't want to spend another minute apart from you."

"It sounds exciting."

"We should definitely do it, and turn it into a country tour with little stops along the way."

"Do you think Christian can spare both of us?"

He collects me in his lap and nips my earlobe. "We won't give him a choice."

Ryan points down at his sketch and goes over his house plans with me. I sigh as I listen to him talk about children and our future.

I am finally creating my happily ever after.

Plucked

After everyone is back on duty, dad returns to his travels and peaceful retirement. And as much as he tries to get Elizabeth to agree to come with him, she stays back with promises to join him soon. As everything settles down, I feel like I can finally breathe.

After the Flu epidemic ends around the country, Karen and Vinny decide to return to the Palace and work until the babies are closer to their due date. And I could not be happier. It is so nice to have Karen close by, and it allows me to be a part of her appointments and maternity care. Vinny is thrilled to come back to work for the Palace, and Christian promotes him to head of the King's guard.

Ryan is always doodling happily on his time off, while I take photos and work on editing them for my portfolio. Together, we are delighted to see what the future holds.

As our trip nears, we finalize the maps and arrangements enthusiastically.

A few days before we leave for our trip, there is a knock on Ryan's door. We both look up as Christian enters.

"Hey, Christian, look at this dorky photo of you. I swear I finally caught you picking your nose. See? I mean, you could be scratching your nose, but I think I can send it to the tabloids and get a pretty penny. Christian? What's wrong?"

"Ann, you need to come with me."

"Is everything okay, Christian?"

He shakes his head and grabs my hand gently. As we walk into the office, everyone watches me and my heart races.

"Please, everyone. Excuse us," Christian says in his stern business-like tone.

I watch Christian fidget and I know something is terribly wrong.

I reach for Ryan's hand, to anchor me for whatever is about to be said.

"Christian, you are scaring me. Please, tell me, what is going on?"

Elizabeth steps forward and I notice tears streaming down her face. She hands me a single piece of paper.

"Ann, I'm so very sorry."

Because of one little sheet of parchment, I am brought to my knees screaming.

The document slides from my fingertips and flutters to my feet. I feel my knees grow weak and I cry in a heap on the ground, as my world crumbles in agony.

With a shaky hand, Ryan, grabs the paper off the floor, and he pales as he kneels beside me stroking my hair. He whispers incoherently as tears stream down his own face.

On the document, it informs the King that my dad's body was found in an abandoned lot—shot and killed.

Thank you

Cliff hangers suck but I promise the answers are coming!

Thank you for reading *Plucked*. What did you think of the book? Could you leave a quick review on Amazon and Goodreads? Just scan the QR code on the next page. Reviews are so important, and I would greatly appreciate it.

I hope you are enjoying Ann's adventure and will continue to read what happens in her life. She is strong and has so much compassion to offer the world.

See Ann again, in all her feathered glory, as she continues her adventure in *Feathered Dreams Book 3: Molting* – coming in 2021!

About the Author

Brittany Putzer was born and raised in Central Florida so the need for sunshine (and coffee) is imbedded in her DNA. Laughing is a must in her world, and she invites her readers to join her.

She always strives for her writing to be quirky, fun, and adventurous. With colorful sprinkles of twists and turns, strong female characters, sweet kisses, and, on occasion, dramatic cliff hangers...

Growing up, she turned to books to escape her real-life obstacles because it was easier to pretend to be a wizard, vampire, or damsel in distress.

Scan the QR code to chat with Brittany on social media, review her book, and join her monthly newsletter.